tha write?

North West England
Edited by Allison Dowse

Disclaimer

Young Writers has maintained every effort
to publish stories that will not cause offence.

Any stories, events or activities relating to individuals
should be read as fictional pieces and not construed
as real-life character portrayal.

Young Writers

First published in Great Britain in 2004 by:
Young Writers
Remus House
Coltsfoot Drive
Peterborough
PE2 9JX
Telephone: 01733 890066
Website: www.youngwriters.co.uk

All Rights Reserved

© Copyright Contributors 2004

SB ISBN 1 84460 600 7

Foreword

Young Writers was established in 1991 and has been passionately devoted to the promotion of reading and writing in children and young adults ever since. The quest continues today. *Young Writers* remains as committed to engendering the fostering of burgeoning poetic and literary talent as ever.

This year, *Young Writers* are happy to present a dynamic and entertaining new selection of the best creative writing from a talented and diverse cross section of some of the most accomplished secondary school writers around. Entrants were presented with four inspirational and challenging themes.

'Myths And Legends' gave pupils the opportunity to adapt long-established tales from mythology (whether Greek, Roman, Arthurian or more conventional eg The Loch Ness Monster) to their own style.

'A Day In The Life Of . . .' offered pupils the chance to depict twenty-four hours in the lives of literally anyone they could imagine. A hugely imaginative wealth of entries were received encompassing days in the lives of everyone from the top media celebrities to historical figures like Henry VIII or a typical soldier from the First World War.

Finally 'Short Stories', in contrast, offered no limit other than the author's own imagination while 'Hold The Front Page' provided the ideal opportunity to challenge the entrants' journalistic skills asking them to provide a newspaper or magazine article on any subject of their choice.

That's Write! North West England is ultimately a collection we feel sure you will love, featuring as it does the work of the best young authors writing today. We hope you enjoy the work included and will continue to return to *That's Write! North West England* time and time again in the years to come.

Contents

Balshaw's CE High School, Leyland
Laura Hodgson (11)	1
Tom Halsall (12)	2
Kate Lancaster-Griffiths (12)	3
Lauren Finch (11)	4
Sam Humphries (12)	5
Andrew Leggett (12)	6
Steven Sanders (12)	7
Daniel Johnson (12)	8
Emma Coupe (12)	10
Samantha Cook (11)	11
Hannah Blundell (11)	12
Micha Waite (12)	13
Kara O'Neill (12)	14
Emily Heaton (12)	15
Chris Owen (12)	16
Holly Oldham (12)	17
Ethan O'Connor (12)	18
Anna Hunkin (12)	19
William Holme (11)	20
Jamie Slater (12)	21
Sherrie Jones (11)	22
Lewis Swarbrick (11)	23

Birkenhead High School, Prenton
Tammy Kahn (14)	24
Siân Holmes (14)	25

Blackpool Sixth Form College, Blackpool
Helen Veasey (17)	26
Amy Croasdale (17)	27
Scott Burnett (16)	28
Jamie Reid (18)	29
Rachel Tsang (17)	30
Victoria Briers (17)	31

Deyes High School, Maghull
Holly Gilligan (13)	32
James Clarke (12)	33
Laura Scaife (17)	34

Ellesmere Port Catholic High School, Whitby
Natalie Harding (12)	38
Rachael Birch (13)	39
Hayley Stephenson (12)	40
Callum Eager (12)	41
Lauren Duffey (12)	42
Charlotte Dowdall (11)	43
Chelsea Bailey (12)	44
Stephanie Atherton (11)	45

Fairfield High School for Girls, Droylsden
Rebecca Marshall (12)	46
Samantha Molloy (12)	47
Hannah Brown (12)	48
Sophia Austin (12)	49
Katherine Barr (12)	50
Samantha Wilbraham (12)	51
Sarah McGuire (12)	52

Kingswood College, Scarisbrick
Sally Devine (12)	53
Jayne Bode (14)	54
Catriona Walker (13)	55

Montgomery High School, Blackpool
Emily Thorley (12)	56
Chelsey Lowenna Clarke (13)	58
Charlotte Darlington (13)	59
Emily Taylor (12)	60
Sally Halliwell (12)	62
Chelsey Cross (13)	63
Joseph Packman (13)	64
Andrea Norton (12)	65
Amanda Jones (12)	66
Michael Scobie (13)	67

Emma Hughes (13)	68
Hannah Walsh (12)	70
Jade Dickinson (12)	71
Daniel McKay (12)	72
Stephen Middleton (13)	73
Jamie Salter (13)	74
Linzi Hull (12)	75

Park High School, Colne

Leanne Moss (13)	76

Pendleton College, Salford

Claire Abbott (16)	80
Sarah Dickerson (16)	82
Joseph Fairhurst (17)	84

Pensby High School for Girls, Wirral

Sarah Trueman (11)	87
Charlotte Collins (11)	88
Olivia McKernan (11)	89
Rebecca Edwards (12)	90
Helen Sheridan (11)	91
Clare Elizabeth Algawi (12)	92
Lisle Taylor (11)	93
Lisa Cunniffe (12)	94
Kimberley Smith (11)	95
Alexandra Power (12)	96
Tasha Stubbs (11)	97
Amy Dallinger (12)	98
Pippa Laurie (12)	100
Stephanie O'Connell (12)	101
Abigayil Thomas (12)	102
Alice Tordoff (11)	103
Alisha Davies (11)	104
Sophie Kirkham (11)	105
Robyn Hall (12)	106

Roundwood High School (MLD), Manchester

Paul Norton (15)	107
Ryan Purdy (14)	108

Thomas Bradley (15)	109
Pamela Wood (15)	110
Graham Neild (15)	111
Luke Cameron (15)	112
Natasha Gasper (14)	113
David Spilsbury (15)	114
Zak Shankland (15)	115

St Bede's RC High School, Blackburn

Bethany Byrom (12)	116
Matthew Tennant (13)	117
Esther Fee (13)	118
Kaitlin King (13)	119
Carly Baldwin (12)	120
Marc Brennan (13)	121
Chris Burt (13)	122
Sarah Cooper (12)	123
Ruth Hartley (13)	124
Rebecca McCann (13)	126
Clare Edwards (13)	127
Gabrielle Wilson (12)	128
Stephanie Hargreaves (13)	129
Chris Hughes (13)	130
Chris Sharples (13)	131
Dominic Marshall (12)	132
Chris Metz (12)	133
Danielle Moore (12)	134
Bianca Castela (12)	136
Simeon Adeoye (12)	137
Emily Davison (13)	138
Laura Summerfield (13)	139
Thomas Miller (11)	140
Bethany Weall (11)	142
Christina Hamill (12)	143
Brydie Kennedy (12)	144
Ryan O'Toole (13)	146
Gemma Coar (12)	147
Erin Finn (12)	148
Megan Ellison (11)	150
James Walsh (11)	151
Gemma Barnes (12)	152

Anna Jackson (12)	153
Hayley McFarlane (11)	154
James Balshaw (12)	156
Jodie McNally (13)	157
Courtney Thomas (11)	158
Samuel Knott (12)	159
Jade Taylor (12)	160
Matthew Hartley (12)	162
Benjamin Yates (11)	163
Jessica Burns (12)	164
Faye Buckley (12)	165
Alex Curran (11)	166
Rhys Dea (12)	167
Anthony Farrell (12)	168
Rebecca Fishwick (11)	169
Dominique Flood (12)	170
Peter Hinnigan (12)	171
Nathan Kennedy (12)	172
Katrina Kenny (12)	173
Robyn Taylor (12)	174
Natalie Peary (11)	175
Ruari McGlone (11)	176
Daniel Eccles (12)	177
Hayley Stanley (12)	178
Elizabeth Mercer (12)	179
Joshua Burke (12)	180
Stevie Walmsley (12)	181
Oliver Houldsworth (11)	182
Nicholas Hoyle (12)	183
Abigail McCann (11)	184
Michaela Gallacher (12)	185
Joseph Smith (12)	186
Polly Hindle (12)	187
Sam McGlynn (12)	188
Katrina Leaf (12)	189
Helen Moore (12)	190
Chelsea Pemberton (11)	191
Matthew Bradley (11)	192
Bianca Whittaker (12)	193
Niall Boyle (12)	194
Francesca Smith (11)	195
Craig Parry (12)	196

Charlotte Matthewman (11) — 197
Callum Boulton (12) — 198
Daisy Boulton (12) — 199

St Chad's Catholic High School, Runcorn
Nomie Clarke (14) — 200
Hazel Clarke (14) — 201
Steff White (14) — 202
Erin Smith (13) — 203
Fern Smith (13) — 204
Lauren Caldwell (14) — 205
Catherine Martin (13) — 206
Alexandra Parkinson (14) — 207
Courtney Reynolds (13) — 208
Raechel Travis (14) — 209
Emma Cattrall (14) — 210
Hayley Meagher (13) — 211
Laura Dixon (14) — 212

Stockport Grammar School, Stockport
Clare Wells (13) — 213
Natalie Ozel (12) — 214

The Creative Writing

A Day In The Life Of A Dog

My day starts at about 7 o'clock when the rest of the family gets up. The baby ignorantly wakes me up by poking me and giving me a hug. I leap up at her, begging her for food. The family have their food before me, but the baby throws me some scraps of bacon. (The food of the gods!) When I get my food, I have roast rabbit Pedigree dog food - *yummy!*

For attention I have to bark. If I want to go for a walk, I usually bark three times. When I actually go for a walk, we usually go to the park (my favourite of all places) where the gushing sound of the waterfall fills the air. The golden sun shines upon me and forms a dark shadow behind me. The sky is as blue as baby Crystal's eyes. Suddenly, a cat as black as soot, shoots past me so I decide to chase it.

When we get home, I beg for my tea. I have to eat leftovers from breakfast - *yes!* When I have finished my delicious meal, I snuggle up in my dog bed and gently fall asleep.

Laura Hodgson (11)
Balshaw's CE High School, Leyland

A Day In The Life Of A Stationery Set

We awoke to the sight of a blinding light, as my master unzipped his pencil case to check that he had everything for the tough day ahead. He zipped us up again and aggressively threw us down the stairs, in the hope that his mother would pick us up and put us in his school bag, next to the cool, draughty door.

We sat there for an hour whilst he ate his breakfast, brushed his teeth, washed his face and put on his blazer. We were then carefully placed on the floor of his car, next to his rugby kit. We set off and braced ourselves for a rough, bumpy journey.

It was now time for the first few lessons. We were all feeling a bit battered and bruised from the ride. Ronald Ruler had even been snapped in half, when the football hit us. It was maths first and it was then that he discovered what had happened to his ruler. He was not happy and neither was his teacher, as she had to lend him one.

The morning was hard and I was glad to hear the bell for lunch break, as I was aching from writing so much. I had been chewed, dropped on the floor and physically tortured. I spent my lunch with - Ronald (still suffering), Eleanor Eraser, Kevin Compass, Penny Protractor and Sammy Setsquare.

It had been a long, hard, challenging day and I was glad to get home! Oh no! Homework!

Tom Halsall (12)
Balshaw's CE High School, Leyland

How The Robin Got Its Wings

One fine Christmas, oh dearest darling, there came a small robin at dear St Nicholas' ear.

'Greetings gentle redbreast, how may I aid thee?' said he.

'It's my Christmas present, sir. I beg you for a pair of wings. At present I cannot fly with my friends, the blue tit, or the sparrow, or the twittering wren.'

Now, you must understand, my love, that in these days, the robin was but a mild, feathered, little thing, with a red breast and a dear voice. He had no wings and this made it a mighty struggle to stay in the air.

'Well,' said St Nick, 'I could maybe solve your problem, although you would have to assist me with something first. Now listen carefully. Each morning at precisely dawn, you are to come and sing to me for three weeks. Should you fail to come, you will get no wings, as this would be breaking a promise and you shall have coal for Christmas.'

Now, the robin was a good animal, so each morning he sang his sweet song and St Nicholas and everyone else agreed that he truly had a marvellous voice. The robin was very proud of his achievement and evermore pleased to be getting his wings.

On Christmas morn, the robin awoke and looked in the mirror and saw, for the first time, his wings! He ran outside and cheered so loud, the whole land awoke and rejoiced, for finally, the robin had wings!

Kate Lancaster-Griffiths (12)
Balshaw's CE High School, Leyland

A Day In The Life Of A Pen

Dear Diary,

It is 8am and I am just waking up. Not that I slept well anyway. Do you know how uncomfortable these shelves are? I think WH Smiths has just opened. I hope all those people don't come smelling me again. I mean, I know I have a shower every morning, but really, are the folk of this town so obsessed with the smell of grape? I should be quite grateful actually, because my friends, (orange, lemon and bubblegum flavoured pens) get thrown about the place all day. People can't even be bothered to put us back on the shelves!

Yesterday I nearly died. Those shopping baskets are so dangerous! I slipped through one of those holes and nearly broke my flippin' nib! The people round here are so careless.

A little five-year-old bought me the day before last. She took me home and nearly suffocated me in one of those stupid plastic bags. Anyway, she scribbled and scribbled, until I felt like I'd practically run a marathon! But that was not all, yesterday she brought me back here and you'll never guess what . . . she said I had *run out!*

I was absolutely gutted. How dare she criticise me like that. Some people are so ungrateful! The shop assistant just rammed a new cartridge inside me (*ouch!*) and plonked me back on the shelf with my old friend Tipp-Ex.

Let's see what today brings!

See you!

Grape the pen.

Lauren Finch (11)
Balshaw's CE High School, Leyland

A Day In The Life Of A Fire

Hello, I'm Fire and here is an example of a normal day for me and many others around the world.

I'm silent, no one can see me, everyone hasn't a clue, they just get on with their daily tasks and then, I'm there! No one seems to notice, so I get so angry that steam is flying off me. Now someone needs to notice me. I get bigger and soon I catch fire to some trees in the wood. Things really start to blaze. The smoke turns thick, black and deadly and I get very angry. I wander around, spreading the inferno everywhere, wondering why no one's noticed me.

In my head I think I can hear sirens, there's flashing lights everywhere and they are wearing masks and yellow helmets. They look at me as if I'm scaring them. They start spraying water at me. I can't live with the freezing temperature, so I try to get away, but they keep following me, it's impossible!

'Help!' I cry. I try to burn more wood and the surroundings. I succeed for a while, but it begins to fail and I get helpless and weak. I start to get frail and I stop running, I stop hiding, I let them take me down and it hits me, somebody noticed me. I was happy, but it was too late to enjoy it, they drove me out and search for pieces of me in the wreckage and I'm gone, gone forever, but my ashes still remain.

Sam Humphries (12)
Balshaw's CE High School, Leyland

A Day In The Life Of A Football

The sun comes up and the football is excited. The thought of flying up in the air is too good to turn down. The excited owner and his friend kick him in the air, he can feel the wind blowing against him. He is then crammed into a bag, along with football boots and shinpads. It's all dark and bumpy in the bag, but when the first crack of light appears, he is as giddy as a clown. The first thing he sees are the two teams and their determined faces. They look at him like a cowboy at an Indian.

The anticipation builds as the whistle blows and then *boot*, he is kicked high into the air. He is soaring like a bird. He is a spinning tornado. He feels dizzy as he hits the back of the net. Once again he is twisting and turning. He is free to do whatever he likes while in the air.

The final whistle blows and a look of disappointment spreads across his face. He is once again put into the dreaded bag on the bumpy journey home.

The only thing that cancels out the disappointment of the day ending, is the fact that it will all happen again tomorrow. He now cuddles up in the back of the net, dreaming of the day he's had.

Andrew Leggett (12)
Balshaw's CE High School, Leyland

The Sword Of Invincibility

Just over two thousand years ago, in the land of ancient Greece, the Roman Empire was threatening to take over their land. A council of mythical beasts decided to make a sword of all the strength and magic of the world. The sword was eventually built, the blade was made from silver and steel mixed together, with symbols painted on with woad. With the handle made from gold, studded with expensive gems and with symbolic engravements.

Then the Romans came, the creatures led their army to the battlefield. There were slashes, bruises, roaring and falling, until a legionnaire, Arthourus, took the sword and kept it in his villa, on top of a stone, in the middle of his fountain. His brother, Arthhexer, wanted the sword for himself, so one night he took the sword from the fountain and fled to Egypt.

Later, he went to a forest to train with the sword, but he had forgotten the sword was magical, it had a life of its own and it summoned a scarab beetle to the forest. Arthhexer tried to fight it, but the sword made him weak. The scarab beetle killed him and disappeared.

Arthourus came and found his dead brother. He took his brother and the sword to the nearest lake. He buried his brother, then took the sword and threw it into the lake, where it has laid ever since, forgotten.

Steven Sanders (12)
Balshaw's CE High School, Leyland

The Life Of A Bike!

Being a bike is not as easy as it seems. I mean, when you go on a bike, you don't realise how much pain and torment it is that you put us through. For example, have you ever been sat on by someone twice as heavy as you? Do you know how it feels to be cramped up all day in a garage or a shed, with other bikes squashing you? I bet all the answers to these questions, in your opinions, would be a straight and simple - no! Well, let me tell you about the worst day of my life.

It all started off on Monday morning, when I woke to the rising sun, to realise that last night I was left in the garden with a big chain around my neck, in the bitter cold. I thought that my owner had abandoned me, but I saw that the shed had been knocked down, which meant that they would be building a new home for me.

Luke, who is my owner, came charging out of the house with a key in his hand, as if he was going to stab someone, only the key was to unlock the chain around my neck. Luke unlocked the chain and with a tremendous thump, jumped onto my back and stood on my hands and started to pedal out of the garden. Getting out of the garden is horrible, as the big sticks and stones get rammed into the gaps in my legs and with Luke sat on your back, it could be the worst moment in your life.

Swerving in and out of cars, Luke headed in a direction where I had never been before.

'Brake!' shouted a man from across the road and so he did, causing most of my skin to fall off my legs, while I skidded to a halt. We had just missed another car, but I think being hit by a car would have been much better, because Luke would have got more hurt than me.

And so we continued up and down all the hills imaginable, with the bones in my legs constantly being changed to different settings. I couldn't help thinking, *where on earth were we going*? I knew I was soon to find out. The journey up to now had been the furthest that I had ever been in my short life. It seemed to be like a never-ending punishment. I didn't understand what I had done wrong. It felt as if he was going to abandon me.

We finally reached our destination, it was where I was made. (Maybe I might see my mum?) Luke jumped off my back and ran in towards the shop. He came back out with a man, who grabbed me by my neck and lifted me up and into the shop. I didn't understand what was going on, but then it hit me like a bullet shot so hard that the man almost dropped me. I realised that my nightmares had come true . . . Luke *was* abandoning me! I felt like screaming, but I couldn't. The only thing on my mind was, *where was I going to go next and who might me my next owner?*

Daniel Johnson (12)
Balshaw's CE High School, Leyland

A Day In The Life Of My Rubber

I lay there, looking up at darkness, then suddenly light poured into my house, blinding me. I saw someone's hand coming down to grab one of us, I didn't know who it would be next. Would it be Mr Pen, lying hopelessly on my right, or even little sharpener on my left? As I thought, it was me, my owner's hand, all sweaty and sticky, grabbed me and pulled me out. I was just quick enough to have got a glance of Miss Ruler's terrified look.

As he dropped me on the table, I thought the worst was over, it obviously wasn't, as I was picked up a second time and rubbed against a piece of paper and I started to lose my hair. He blew all my hair off the table! I watched as it dropped to the floor.

I could tell he was getting annoyed with me, as he continuously rubbed me again and again. I was very hot and suddenly, my owner's friend picked me up and started rubbing vigorously against some paper. That was all soon over.

I heard a bell ring, it was the end of the lesson. I got picked up, thrown back into my home and into his bag. I prepared myself for another lesson of rubbing out.

Emma Coupe (12)
Balshaw's CE High School, Leyland

A Day In The Life Of Zoe Zoom (6012 Future Kid)

Hello vintage child!

I'm Zoe Zoom. I was born on the 15th of January 6000. It's now the 29th of November 6012, so that means I'm twelve years old. I'm writing this because I know you're only in 2004 now, so I thought it would be interesting for you to know what it's like now . . .

Firstly, my family and me. There's me - full name Zoe Anne Zoom, my two brothers, Zee (14) and Zed (12) (both annoying!) my two sisters Zara (16) and Zena (8) and my mum and dad, Zack and Zelda, both 40 and still really healthy.

Secondly, changes. We have only changed by lip and eye colour. Our lips are now blue and our eyes are either black and white, red and purple, or green and yellow! I suppose we are evolving in small ways, all the time! Clothes, toys, food and shops haven't changed, except for car shops, because cars are now 6m off the ground!

Currently, I don't go to school. I have HTC (home tutoring system) to teach me. Basically, it's a computer with a virtual teacher in it! When I go to college, I'm not allowed to use a HTC.

I'll send this in my TS I got for Christmas. It sends things to a different era in a flash!

Well, hope you get this letter!

Love Zoe Anne Zoom xxx.

Samantha Cook (11)
Balshaw's CE High School, Leyland

A Day In The Life Of An Egyptian Slave

Today I was woken up at 6am with a whip lashing at my back. It stung for hours afterwards. My wife and I have to carry blocks of stone to the hill on the other side of the desert. The children had to carry smaller pieces of stone, but it was still just as hard for them, as it was for us. We were forced not to stop and even if we stopped to wipe the sweat that was dripping from our faces, we got whipped until we could not take it any longer. The day was getting hotter and hotter and so the work was getting harder and harder every second.

During the middle of the day, some new slaves came. They had only been there for about half an hour and they were working as hard as the older ones were. They were not used to this type of treatment being used on them, so they were upset and angry, they were sweating and aching too.

For our food we got the same as usual, a slice of bread and a cup of water. The children got a cup of water and two slices of bread.

Today had been the hottest day of the year, so the Egyptians watched us working whilst they lay and sunbathed. All this feels like torture, but we have done nothing wrong. Why do the Egyptians hate us so much? What have we done to deserve this slavery that we are being forced to do?

Hannah Blundell (11)
Balshaw's CE High School, Leyland

Odysseus And The Sirens

Odysseus and his crew were sailing near the island of the Sirens - bewitching singers who enchanted every man who came near them. If a man heard their song, he would never go back home, because the Sirens' song would draw him in. Around them were heaps of dead bodies with shrivelling skin and rotting organs.

Odysseus' friend, Circe, had told him how to safely pass the Sirens, so he stowed away the sail and took out the oars. He took a big ball of wax, split it and blocked his comrades' ears with it. But he wanted to hear the Sirens' song, so he had his men tie him to the ship's mast. Then they rowed.

When the ship got near to the Sirens' island they began to sing; 'Draw near to us, famous Odysseus, most glorious hero; anchor your ship and listen to our voices! No man has yet passed by in his dark ship, without listening to the sweet song that comes from our mouths and rejoicing at it. For we know all about the tales of the Achaens and Trojans at Troy; and we know all that comes to pass on the rich Earth.'

Odysseus wanted to listen so badly, he told his comrades to set him free. However, they realised he was only acting upon the Sirens' song and bound him more tightly. So when they had rowed clear of this island, the men took the wax out of their ears and carried on with their journey.

Micha Waite (12)
Balshaw's CE High School, Leyland

A Day In The Life Of A Victorian Street Urchin

My name is Charlie. This is the diary of my life, only I don't have much of a life. I live on the streets with my two younger brothers. My parents died from pneumonia and I fear that both myself and my brothers will die soon. We have no money, nor food.

We have always been poor. When he was alive, my father spent all of our money on drink. I hated my father. He would belt me for no reason, sometimes 5 or 10 times. He was worse when he was drunk. It sounds wicked, but I'm glad he died. As for my mother, she never stood up to him. I could hear her at night crying, while he was out drinking. My mother was never a strong person. My father often beat her too. If she seemed distracted on Sundays while reading the Bible, he would belt her and make her confess her sins at church, making them seem more terrible than they actually were.

Now we have no future. My brothers and I are ill and homeless. We were put into an orphanage, but we played truant and got thrown out. We hated it there anyway. We resorted to pick-pocketing and got caught red-handed by the Peelers. All three of us got a clip round the ear. It was quite a whack! It brought back terrible memories of my father. I suppose I am going where my father is. He always said I would go to Hell . . .

Kara O'Neill (12)
Balshaw's CE High School, Leyland

A Day In The Life Of A Schoolbag

What does she think she's doing? She can't go to school without me! I am carrying her vital geography project, which needs handing in today and I don't want to sit listening as her geography teacher launches into his 'this is just not good enough . . .' speech. Hooray! She's finally remembered - but does she have to drag me across the floor like this?

Great! We're in physics and the teacher's droning on about the solar system and how great the first man on the moon was! But no one ever mentions the bag that accompanied him all the way there. No one ever mentions the bag that carried all of the emergency kit, the bag which made sure 'the first man on the moon' came back safely!

Break, well this is my favourite part of the day. (I don't think!) Go ahead - throw me on the floor then; don't bother thinking about my feelings. *Ouch!* Why do people always aim balls at bags? It's as if they think we don't have feelings too! Now, that is just disgusting . . . who just threw crisps all over me? And why do they always have to be cheese and onion? (I'll stink for days!) I hate the way school kids abandon their bags.

Look who it is, he's always in trouble. *Oi!* what do you think you're doing? Get out, I'm not your bag! He's scarpered with the geography project . . . it's in the bin. Bring on the 'this is just not good enough . . .' speech and . . . *detention!*

Emily Heaton (12)
Balshaw's CE High School, Leyland

A Day In The Life Of A Farmer's Field

The sun rises in the east and the dew glistens on the blades of grass covering the farmer's field, like stars shimmering in the midnight sky. Dawn is upon us, as the cockerel awakens the dreamers of the farm.

I am disturbed from my calm contentment, by a silent, swishing wind slapping me in my face. My friends are knocked with force, like a football being kicked. The pack awakens and suddenly there is life on the farmer's field. There is no breakfast, lunch or even dinner, just silence all through the day. Then that silence is broken by the deafening howl of the tractor in the farmer's grasp. He whistles while he works, to the beat of the tractor's engine.

As the farmer works, I gaze at the birds swooping over me, looking for field mice and other prey, like aeroplanes flying low over your heads. What's this I see climbing up my blade? It's a ladybird, all colourful and spotty. Its little delicate legs tickle my blade as it reaches my peak. The farmer stretches for his sunglasses, but I have nothing to shield me from the sun's glare. The farmer protects his skin with cream, but my blades lack shelter from the sun's harmful rays and soon become brown and scorched.

The farmer switches off his engine and sits down for his lunch. Ramblers stroll across the perimeter of my field, with their dogs sniffing curiously at the wilderness that surrounds them. The farmer begins his work again, by rounding up the cows, ready to be milked. As they come nearer, they trample over me and turn up the ground, dropping enormous cowpats all over the field. They enter the cowshed and silence is upon us again.

As dusk draws nearer the atmosphere changes. The sky darkens, the birds sing, the nocturnal animals come out from their hiding places and havoc begins. The wolf howls, the sheep baa, the owl hoots, the mice squeak and me, well I just watch and wonder as the night begins again . . .

Chris Owen (12)
Balshaw's CE High School, Leyland

A Day In The Life Of A Pound Coin

I emerged from a machine at the Royal Mint in London. I took my first breath as I moved down a chute to be bagged up and taken to the bank.

Suddenly, I fell into the huge bag. It was dark inside. The bag was then hurled into a big truck and we started moving. We must have travelled for hours, but we eventually pulled up at a bank somewhere in Preston. We were taken out of the truck and into the bank. The truck driver left.

One of the cashiers from the bank came and opened the bag. At last we saw daylight again! A lady's hand appeared in the bag and pulled out some coins, again she reached in, she pulled me out, she took me to a safe and locked it, we were in darkness again! I nearly suffocated under all the other pound coins, but I survived.

I must have done because the safe opened and I was taken out along with some other coins. I was carried to a desk where somebody was waiting. The lady handed me over to the person. She put me into her jacket pocket.

Then I was on my travels again. I was jingling around in her pocket. To the side of me I heard a voice, 'Got any change, Missus?' The next thing I knew, I was tossed into the hat.

Holly Oldham (12)
Balshaw's CE High School, Leyland

The Evil Seeker

I never believed in magic, well not real magic at least, until one day about three months ago, I was forced to. My father told me that our family was a generation unlike no other, we were seekers and that our family had been growing stronger for centuries, until the one true seeker would defeat all evil everywhere and that seeker was me! I didn't believe him. I mean, how many 12-year-old seekers do you know?

Just a few hours later, I was on my way home from the graveyard, which I've visited regularly ever since my mum died, just six months earlier, when I was attacked by some kind of creature. It stood like a human, but her face was all distorted. She had fangs like a vampire, white hair and strange, tribal markings down her arms and face. She wore a leather crop top, that looked like it had been ripped with her talons. Her long, black, ripped skirt trailed behind her.

She jumped at me and instantly I kicked at her. She must have propelled back at least 25 feet and landed on a car, smashing the windscreen to pieces. Instinct told me to fly forwards. I landed on the car above her and out of nowhere, a sharp, jewelled knife appeared in my hand and I stabbed her. She vanished.

I don't know where these powers come from, but I know I must use them to avenge my mother's death and prevent the spread of these creatures.

Ethan O'Connor (12)
Balshaw's CE High School, Leyland

Ranchoz The Lion

Ranchoz was a lion. A lion with a heart. He wanted to help everyone he met, especially little animals. The problem was, nobody knew he was kind and helpful and as soon as they saw him, they ran. Ran and ran till the blisters on their blisters popped. Ranchoz wanted this to change.

One glorious day, the sun was shining and the leaves on the jungle trees glistened. Ranchoz strolled out of his den looking for trouble. This may seem weird, but he wasn't actually looking to start trouble, he was looking to help someone out of it. On he strolled, nobody was in sight. 'Please come out someone,' he moaned to himself. 'Please!' Still he searched, but he couldn't see anyone at all. He finally decided to go home to his den.

Ranchoz sat and thought. How could he find someone to help? Then it hit him, he needed to go far into the jungle where the little animals lived.

The very next day, Ranchoz set out on his journey. He had to keep stopping, because it was such a long way. When he arrived there, he saw a mouse being backed into a rock, by a panther. Over Ranchoz strolled. *'Roar!'* he yelled, with all his might. 'Get away from that helpless mouse, you evil beast!'

The panther trembled at the knees and ran with all his strength through the jungle, like a sports car.

'Thank you!' yelped the mouse. 'Thank you so much! I must spread the word, Ranchoz is the kindest lion in the world.'

'Thank you!'

Anna Hunkin (12)
Balshaw's CE High School, Leyland

A Day In The Life Of My Cat

It all started on a normal, average Saturday morning.

I was having my usual bowl of cornflakes, like I do every week. As I switched the television on, my cat, Shiraz, entered the room and dashed into his cat litter. The next thing I knew, I was in the cat litter! I thought I was dreaming and when I tried to pinch myself, I couldn't because I didn't have any fingers, just paws with a lot of hair on them! I was very confused, so I tried to sit down, but then I wished I hadn't because I ended up sitting in a big pile of cat mess.

As I went out of the litter tray, I felt so tempted to lick my bum, but luckily I didn't because my mum came into the kitchen, saw the mess on my back and threw me outside. It was raining so I ran for shelter. I ran under a bush, but I still got wet. I remembered that my bedroom window was open, so I went to the front of the house and stood under my window. I thought to myself I would never make it. I crouched down and then I jumped. It felt so amazing and before I knew it, I was back in the house and in my room.

I ran downstairs and back into the kitchen. I hit the door and all of a sudden, I was back in my chair, eating my breakfast.

William Holme (11)
Balshaw's CE High School, Leyland

Being A Hamster

Oh, I wish they wouldn't clean me out! I don't like that new smell, it's horrible! I like my smell, it's nice. What are you doing? *Ouch!* That hurts, get off, stop poking me. If you're trying to tickle my belly, it's not working, you're just making my angry. You're asking for it, I'll bite you. I mean it, although now I have some teeth I need some . . . some . . . *sniff, sniff, sniff,* oh, what's that I smell? It smells like . . . *erm* . . . smells like breakfast and it's dried hamster food from Harries. Only for Russian dwarfs. Yes, I do like Harries, especially those red hamster chews. Anyhow, no matter, let's eat!

Yum, well, that just filled me up, time to run on my wheel just for that little bit of exercise. Oh no, not again. Stop picking me up. Hey! Where are you taking me? Get me out of here! I hate this blue plastic bowl! Yeah! You better take me out!

Oooh! This is comfy, nice, new bedding, *yawn*, I am tired, might just take a, *yawn,* small nap. What the . . .?

It's morning, no one woke me. Oh, the cheek of it! When I want to sleep in they wake me and when I just want a small nap, what do they do? *Nothing!*

I hate my life!

Jamie Slater (12)
Balshaw's CE High School, Leyland

Lucky Laura Wins Lottery!

19-year-old from Leyland becomes millionaire!

Last night 19-year-old Laura Oldham won £8,749,000 on the National Lottery, though unlike most teenagers she doesn't plan on dropping out of university and buying whatever she wants.

'I've heard of people who let the money take over their lives, but I'll never let that happen. The money will pay off my university fees, buy my parents a new house and a car for myself. The rest I'm going to save for when I'm older and know what to spend it on'.

Her friends and family are over the moon with her decision and told us they're proud that she's so mature. When she found out she'd won, she was at her friend Kara's house. They decided to watch the show during a break in studying and screamed the house down when they discovered the news!

'I expected her to start reeling off a list of things she would buy', commented Kara, 'but she didn't, I screamed at her, what are you going to buy? She just said, 'Nothing'. I respect her for that'.

Another young winner, Rebecca Cuthbertson, said she let the money take over her life and although she now lives in a 4.5 million pound mansion, she hates life.

'People are so hungry for the money, I must admit I was too, though I hate the money now. Laura seems a very mature woman, but you never know what might happen'.

Sherrie Jones (11)
Balshaw's CE High School, Leyland

The Legend Of Actez

Many years ago there lived a man named David. David lived with his father King Kanus and his two brothers, Angus and Farimier. One day, David was just sitting down for his lunch with the family, when one of Kanus' guards interrupted the meal for an urgent announcement.

He said, 'Lord Kanus, we have horrific news. There is a beast that's been sighted near the town and people are protesting, and will, until it is slayed.'

'Very well,' said the king, 'one of the best soldiers will be sent to slay the beast. My son, David, shall slay this so-called beast to show the people that David has the bravery to be the next king.'

David sat gobsmacked, as he looked in fear at his father.

The next morning, David set out the weapons he would use to slay the beast. He had a spear, a knife, a sword and a shield. His father came out and placed on him the legendary gold plated armour. David took one huge gulp and set off down the road.

David found out that the beast was named Actez and lived at the top of a mountain in a cave. David set off up the mountain towards the cave and soon reached the cave and found Actez, the beast, asleep. David snuck in and as the beast was slowly awakening, David plunged in his sword and slayed Actez.

When David returned, he returned to a happy party and was crowned King David of Greece.

Lewis Swarbrick (11)
Balshaw's CE High School, Leyland

An Ideal World

Do you remember reading fairy tales of bravery and heroism? Reading the famous happy endings of perfection and wishing you were part of that happiness? Wishing that instead of helplessly staring at the smiles and running your finger over the picture, you could jump into the book and leave everything you hate about the world behind. I live in that fairy-tale ending. A loving mother and father who would always be there to catch me when I fall and a twin who shares every moment of my life, who is my best friend . . . no, closer than a best friend, closer than a sister, she is part of me. Our souls are like a needlework, each moment of our lives together is another stitch in the pattern, tying us closer to one another. Even our fairy-tale house is unable to be touched by any of the evil realities that change so many people's lives.

I live in a world of perfection, where nothing goes wrong and no one feels the daggers of pain, the short, sharp gasps of unhappiness. What more could I ask for?

The crumpled figure of a girl sat scrunched in the corner, her hands over her ears, blocking out the silence of an empty house. Still staring at the wall, as if concentrating hard enough would take her out of this prison. She was alone and as she sat rocking backwards and forwards, the pages of her book fell to the floor.

Tammy Kahn (14)
Birkenhead High School, Prenton

Going Stateside

The phrase, 'like mother, like daughter' has been used appropriately on many occasions. There is a time and a place for this saying and that time and place was not Saturday morning in the Smith household.

Upstairs, in Katherine's bedroom, the usual, uplifting shaft of Saturday morning sunlight was beaming through the gap in-between the closed, purple curtains and then reflecting off the slightly dusty mirror at the other end of the room and then directly into one of the emerald-green eyes belonging to Katherine Smith. Kat was lying half-awake, half-asleep in her bed, having just been woken up by her hamster, Derek, who had decided to go for a run on his (very noisy) hamster wheel, before he went to bed. After all, hamsters are nocturnal, but it was a small price to pay for Kat who loved him to bits. Which was more than could be said for how she felt about her mother, Pam.

Pam Smith was a middle-aged 'mutton dressed as lamb' control freak of a mother. Over the years, Pam had turned jealous of her daughter and became obsessed with having authority over her. She started drinking, staying out late and leaving Kat alone in the evenings, while she went 'down the pub'.

Many a day Kat and Pam argued like cat and dog; usually over the same things, over and over again. But one thing in particular; how much Kat wanted to go and live with her father, Stateside.

Siân Holmes (14)
Birkenhead High School, Prenton

The Bride

It was the morning of January 9th 2004 and Sarah's big day had arrived, she was getting married to Dave. Dave and Sarah had been together for just over two years and Dave had proposed over a romantic meal in a swish restaurant called Ecuador, where everyone took their partners to propose. I, of course, was chief bridesmaid.

When Sarah finally woke up, she started panicking straight away about everything. It took me and the other bridesmaids two hours to calm her down and have something to drink. After this, we started getting Sarah ready for the day ahead. Finally Sarah was ready and all we had to do was wait for the cars, ours came first, so we wished Sarah good luck and set off to the church in the middle of the village.

We arrived at the church and everyone was standing outside, waiting to go in and be shown where they would be seated. Sarah arrived in a classic Rolls Royce. As she climbed out, her dress shone like a beacon of light in the sun, she looked amazing in her white, flowing dress. She was like a fairy princess, turning up for her winter ball.

As Sarah started towards the church, the bridesmaids fell in line behind her, forming a procession of women in beautiful dresses. Little did we know that disaster was about to strike. As our beaming friend reached the end of the path . . . she fell flat on her face!

Helen Veasey (17)
Blackpool Sixth Form College, Blackpool

The Bribe

Melissa rushed in the door and slammed it hard behind her. 'I hate that Mr Pimery so much, he is so stupid!'

Gillian was one of those mothers that hated to see their children upset, so she decided to do something about it. She pulled out a box from under her bed.

'What are these?' Melissa asked curiously.

'These are pictures of our Mr Pimery, with someone he shouldn't be with,' she replied suspiciously.

Gillian searched for the perfect picture to send with a truly twisted letter.

'This is it, Mum,' Melissa found it, 'he wouldn't want this to get around, trust me.'

Melissa wished that she could have seen his face when he opened it and the sordid photo fell out onto his lap and the harsh sense of reality hit him *hard*.

A hand grabbed her in the corridor, it seemed to come from nowhere. 'What are you playing at? You won't get away with this.'

'I have no idea what you're talking about, Sir,' she replied innocently, although there was nothing innocent about *her*.

'OK,' he said, 'I'll give you what you want, you have the award, but I want all the photos and negatives in return.'

Melissa agreed and they made a deal. Gillian wasn't happy about handing over the photos and negatives, but at least her daughter got the award that she thought she deserved.

Amy Croasdale (17)
Blackpool Sixth Form College, Blackpool

The Machine

I was out with my mum shopping for my birthday present. As we passed an arcade, we decided to pop in and have a little flutter. I looked around and the arcade was selling all the machines. I saw one that drew me towards it, it was a truth telling machine. I decided to buy it with my birthday money. I got it delivered at my house for half-past five, an hour before my party was planned for. I anxiously waited for my friends to arrive.

They finally arrived and began playing on the machine straight away. However, the weird thing was, that all the cards had a certain time on them. It was 10pm, but it was only 9.50. All my friends weren't particularly bothered about it, but I was. As the clock hit 10, I saw my friend Rob collapse onto the floor, people rushed around him, but they could not stir him. Then, everyone else started to fall to the floor as well. They lay there unconscious. I believed it to be the machine from the arcade. As I was looking over to my friends, a thought came to me, *are they dead or just sleeping?* I couldn't help wondering what was going to happen to me.

Scott Burnett (16)
Blackpool Sixth Form College, Blackpool

The Death Of Ruikayé

As ten o'clock approached, the night was beginning to seem like it would never end. Being a friend's 18th birthday, it would not be polite to just leave early, so we were in it until the bitter end. The entire evening was filled with cheap food from the buffet, cheap alcohol and even cheaper music. Every once in a while, a karaoke act was thrown in, the synthesised sounds which supported a painfully dreary vocal performance, made the evening even harder to bear.

Walking around, I was constantly being introduced to my friend's relatives and found myself in uncomfortable situations after the initial 'hello'.

Ruikayé, which were two friends who had decided to form a team, made their mark over the evening. Drink after drink their confidence was slowly building up and they had already made several karaoke requests.

The night had had its share of violence and stupid antics, but at around 11.30, the last karaoke act was announced. Ruikayé were to finish off the night's entertainment. They took the stage and shared a few private jokes as a crowd formed. The music for Westlife's 'Mandy' began to play and the two of them began to sing.

When the song ended, the crowd's reaction showed everyone's disapproval of the performance and on that night, Ruikayé's deluded fantasy of success in music, ended. After the performance, Ruikayé seemed angry and every little incident aggravated them. They had gotten into two fights over the course of the evening. Both had also lost their girlfriends and they left the party with nothing.

In one night, the two most irritating pair of 'comedians', were reduced to nothing, as they quickly found out that they weren't funny.

Jamie Reid (18)
Blackpool Sixth Form College, Blackpool

The Car

It was summertime in Britain and we were driving on the M6 in my brand new car. 'You guys been up to much?' I asked.

'Working mostly,' Jed replied. Jed was an undergraduate student, an intelligent, laid-back guy.

The speed dial displayed 70mph. I pressed on the brakes, but the speed dial still read 70mph. Just my imagination. I pressed even harder on the brakes now, but still the car wasn't slowing down. I realised the brakes weren't functioning and before I knew it, we were behind a fast-moving coach. Panic suddenly spread over my entire body.

I once again tried to push on the brakes, hoping somehow they would begin to function again, but no luck. I could feel my hands getting sweaty and I was suddenly short of breath and my heart pounded harder against my ribcage, I could hear it. I could see the frightened looks on all my friends' faces and none of us spoke.

I wished somehow that it was just a horrible nightmare, but it wasn't. I tried to think, but all I could think about, was my friends and I crashing. There was no way of escaping this one, unless . . .

Rachel Tsang (17)
Blackpool Sixth Form College, Blackpool

The Wait

Tick-tock, tick-tock is all I can hear whilst sitting eagerly awaiting nine o'clock to receive the results, results which would, to me, determine my whole future and where I would be spending the next few years. If I would be spending it creating huge debts for myself, getting completely drunk, oh and getting a bit of an education too.

I've been waiting for this day for weeks. Now it's here, I'm not so sure! I'm praying for BBB and today is the day I find out.

As I walk down the hall to the room, on my way I pass a variety of people, either crying and being consoled or jumping up with glee, having received what they were hoping for.

I then approach a small lady with long hair and far too much make-up on! She had a very harsh voice and looked as if she didn't really want to be there. She asked for my name, 'Jane Gompson,' I replied. She handed me a plain, white envelope. As I took the envelope, I felt my stomach turning, my heart pumping so much, I thought it would burst, my hands were shaking and I was sweating, nervously. As I opened the envelope and took out the paper, my heart stopped for a second as I read my results: BBU. I felt like crying and that I had fallen into a downward spiral of depression and darkness from which I would never escape. Or would I?

Victoria Briers (17)
Blackpool Sixth Form College, Blackpool

Midsummer's Day
(Inspired by 'His Dark Materials' trilogy by Philip Pullman)

It was Midsummer's Day, 11.40am. Lyra traced the familiar steps through the botanic garden. She went past the pool with a fountain under a wide-spreading tree, turned left and walked between beds of plants, towards a huge, many-trunked pine. Past the large stone wall with a doorway in it, through the less formal part of the garden, where the planting is younger. Lyra went almost to the end of the garden, over a little bridge and sat down on a wooden seat, under a spreading, low-branched tree.

Lyra looked at her watch, 11.55am, she breathed a sigh of relief and called Pan to her, he ran to the bench and jumped onto her lap.

In Will's Oxford, in the botanic garden, on that same wooden seat, he felt a shiver run down his spine. His heart leapt, his stomach clenched and he knew that, in a sense, Lyra had just sat down next to him. Kirjava skulked up to him and he stroked her ears absent-mindedly, for he was thinking of Lyra. The way her fingers touched his mouth when she gently put the little red fruit inside it. The way their lips clumsily bumped together as they kissed, how every fibre of their beings was ablaze with love and adoration.

The church clock chimed midday, though neither man nor woman heard, for they were too lost in the past.

Holly Gilligan (13)
Deyes High School, Maghull

The Life Of King Henry VIII

King Henry VIII lived a peaceful, but dramatic life, hunting, drinking, dancing and gambling.

When people think of him, they say, 'He was married to six wives, executed two, divorced two, one had an illness and one lived on when he died.'

Henry was born in 1491 and died in 1547. Aged 55 he came to the throne in 1509. He was tall, handsome and good at hunting and jousting. He was devoted to his new wife, Catherine of Aragon and he soon found a loyal minister in Thomas Wolsey, whom he made Lord Chancellor.

But Henry wanted a son to succeed him and was prepared to stop at nothing to get his own way. He grew tired of Catherine, who had given him a daughter, Mary. He wanted to marry a woman called Anne Boleyn.

Henry broke with the Pope and the Catholic Church. He married Anne Boleyn, (and divorced Catherine soon afterwards) became Supreme Head of the English Church and destroyed the monasteries, because he wanted their wealth. Henry dealt ruthlessly with those who opposed him. Few people close to him, especially his wives, escaped trouble.

The old Henry was a terrifying, old figure. Henry VIII married six times and his wives suffered various fates. They were: Catherine of Aragon (divorced), Anne Boleyn (beheaded), Jane Seymour (died), Anne of Cleves (divorced), Catherine Howard (beheaded) and Katherine Parr (survived). He had three children: Mary I (daughter of Catherine of Aragon), Elizabeth I (daughter of Anne Boleyn) and Edward VI (son of Jane Seymour).

James Clarke (12)
Deyes High School, Maghull

Run On Girl

The beginning marked a new point in my life. It broke the boundaries between fiction and reality: it changed my world.

I was half a mile away from home. The time of year that I enjoyed best had finally arrived, winter. Those old autumn leaves clung to the bottom of my shoes, leaving an uncomfortable feeling underfoot. Car tyres crunched down the road, then stopped at red lights. I stared and wondered what these people were like: some were fantastically dynamic, others were just content with plodding by. Before the news that changed my world, I was the former, but my life was about to be different.

The journey passed in an uneventful haze; the next thing I remembered was a key pushing into a lock, then the door slowly opening; it didn't feel right. I was about to find out that nothing was the same; it had all changed.

Where's my coffee? Where's Mum? How come it's so quiet? Maybe I knew. My brother had been sent for tests at The Royal that morning: MRI scans, EEG scans and hopefully to conclude the business, a positive diagnosis.

'How's Scott?'

There was no response, just incoherent muffling from behind a scrunched up hankie. 'Well,' my mother drew breath and with what seemed like a great effort, continued to talk, 'you know he went for that scan today,' she exhaled, then screwed up her eyes. Whatever this was, it was costing her to say, 'It's bad, it's a tumour, they think . . .'

It was too late. I had already switched off to the clinical ranting. My stomach lurched. How could she phrase it so childishly? This was more than 'bad'. I felt a stab in my side for being angry with her and a second stab for being so selfish. I knew my mother needed to talk about it, but I couldn't face the tear-stained, blotchy face. I had to get out. I needed to run away, but all my legs would allow me, was to saunter up the stairs, as if to a mournful tune. I flung the door of my room open and made for the bed. Roughly I drew the curtains and then spread myself out across the duvet; the sweet, powdery smell brought some comfort, but couldn't offer any sympathy. My head was filled with an angry buzz; I swallowed hard, *what if he dies?* I couldn't bear to say his name: it made it too real. A friend once told me, talking about your problems could clarify a situation; I asked, did it work for butter? But they said no, just the soul.

I needed to escape my thoughts, as they were suffocating me; without consideration I inched away from the bed and crouched as far in the corner as I could. This was a bad dream. A very, bad dream.

I wanted to forget the last fifteen months, but how could I? I remembered everything. I remembered his forgetfulness, his dislike of loud music and that pitiless day when his mind wouldn't allow him to dredge up my name. These memories were etched on the landscape of my life, cruel reminders that nature doesn't favour the good.

The rain beat down, hard and grey. I watched behind green eyes and clung to my shirt. I felt my hands trembling, felt the sweat on my palms, then I heard Scott cough and Mum call from downstairs. I went out of my room and looked down at her.

'Wake him up, Di.'

The thought of entering the room filled me with dread. When I closed the door to my room, I thought I had disappeared, but I hadn't and it looked as if life had to go on. I knocked on the door and called softly, 'Scott?' No answer. That churning thought came back to me, *is he OK?* I opened the door. He was there. He didn't acknowledge me, just sat there; this was unnerving. His eyes shone.

There was nothing behind them when he looked at me, so silently, I left him and entered my room, my space with its familiar smell and childish relics. I was scared and starting to get angry again. I was tired and hungry and damp from my journey home. I just couldn't hold on anymore. I burst into tears, great gulpy sobs, like a baby.

Footsteps padded up the stairs; I knew they were coming for me, maybe I wanted them to. I waited for Mum to get angry, tell me my selfish ways had to end and only our strength would get Scott through. She looked at me; it was like she was looking right through my eyes into my head and all the worries inside.

'Oh Di,' she sighed, as if all the breath had been kicked out of her. 'Oh Di, why has it happened to us?'

When we broke from our embrace, I realised that the phone was ringing. Ringing and ringing. It was Annabelle, my beloved aunt, the person I aspired to be at the age of five, strong, passionate about literature and at this point, emotionally distraught. Life was cruel. It had denied her the joy of children, so she settled for the position of favourite aunt. This was the talk Mum had needed and the one I never wanted to be part of. It was dangerous to discuss what ifs in my opinion, but they did and I heard them all.

What if he needs chemo? What if it's radiotherapy they use? Theresa lost her fingernails and hair when she had it. They said he had - what was it - *temporal lobe epilepsy; induced by swelling due to the size of the tumour and the pressure it put on his brain.*

I couldn't listen to it anymore and so, I moved up to the landing, far enough away to still hear what they were saying, but distant enough to pretend it wasn't real. Up until this point, I had wallowed in death and now, after listening through the banisters, I was left to loiter in the merciless cruelty the next few months could bring. I couldn't think. I didn't want to, but there was nowhere to escape, except the bathroom, so I went there.

I turned on the taps and watched the water whirl from them, then liberally poured all manner of soaps and scents into the crystal pool. I hated the way the bubbles clung to your hair when bath products had been in the water, but I didn't care. I had to get the stench of helplessness off, that clung to my very being. I tested the warm liquid with the tip of my toe, then slowly I edged in, till it covered me. A thought struck me, *what if I delved into the water till I was totally covered: face, mouth, nose? Would my mind then be clear, or body and soul gone forever?* A strange sensation came over me, like pins on my body, rhythmically pricking and stabbing. I couldn't do it. My hair fanned out, as if to recreate a Shakespearean tragedy. I never allowed myself to think of this incident again. Was I surprised by my actions, or sick? I couldn't tell. As I lay in my coffin-shaped tub, I began to consider the enormity of my situation. I could see no end to it and the beginning was so long ago, that I couldn't remember it starting. All I knew was Scott had a tumour growing inside his head, taking over his life, like some omnipotent keeper and we were left wondering, hoping, crying and praying it would find another little figure to destroy.

The water grew cold and I began to shiver. I wondered, was it possible to feel discomfort of the physical kind anymore, when a dull ache of mental anguish held my attention so firmly? I had penetrated deep into the dark corners of my psyche. Did I really feel so bad or was I just living this crisis through the pages of a novel? Could I decipher between illusion and realism anymore? Such unexpected news hurt me terribly, but I could control the melodrama that seemed synonymous with aged Hollywood stars, because I knew I had to.

I felt renewed in the bath; it was taking away a layer of my spirit, like the dead matter it was, the water was hungry for more and I felt free. Slowly, I sat up, allowing the groove of my spine to rub against the plastic. The pressure of the fluid couldn't crush me anymore, the burden of dejection was lifted: life had to go on. We had to help Scott; I had to ignore my own troubles and push my own uncertainties down, as deep as they would go, straight into my soul. I sighed with renewed relief.

Diana Hunt is drowning and there's nothing she can do.

Laura Scaife (17)
Deyes High School, Maghull

A Day In The Life Of A Malaysian Fish

I've just woken up, because of the shoal of cuttlefish making their way to school. They're so noisy, about 200 of them altogether. Anyway, I crawl lazily over to my underwater bathroom to clean my toes, which is a very painful experience.

I emerge full of life and bounce cheerfully to my wooden wardrobe to pick my clothes. In the end, I choose a pink skirt and a purple halterneck top. I can't be bothered to go to work today, but I suppose I better had.

I run happily to my cerise sea horsey, which is a cart pulled by a massive, pinky-purple sea horse. It's quite an amazing sight to you, what d'ya call 'em, pink, hairy things? Hugmans. That's them.

It is beautiful really, looking at my home town, all the bright coloured fish and lights, it's so friendly, every fish helping others, it's a really good environment.

I arrive at my underground laundry shop. There, standing all alone, crying, is Chantel. We go inside and figure out that Dipsy the shark has burgled all the washing liquid.

At once I jump back on my sea horse and ride to the dark side of the sea. I frantically search for Dipsy, I can't see him anywhere. This is a proper big disaster! No washing liquid, no laundry! I pick up the pace, but can't find the evil shark.

Even still to this day, we never did find that shark. But everything turned out all right. My typical day!

Natalie Harding (12)
Ellesmere Port Catholic High School, Whitby

A Day In The Life Of An Endangered Animal

Ssshh! Can you hear it? The shallow whispers of them. Hunters. They're looking for me again. I must protect my family. Their dark spots are hiding them against the bare vegetation. Still. They're moving, they're leaving, we're safe. We're free. For now. If it wasn't for our luxurious fur and the healing powers of our bones, we'd be safe forever.

Now we have to hunt too, for food. Quick, there's one! Briskly, yet hushed, I lurch across to the wild sheep, who is so far, oblivious to my presence. I must take care to catch my prey, as it's been three days since we last ate. Wild sheep and our other source of nourishment, the wild goat, are also becoming rare. Got it! I slowly sink my sharp teeth and my ever-growing claws into its back and I take large chunks of skin when I draw them back out. I've done it. It's no longer alive. I take it aside to the family and they rip it apart and at last, they have feasted.

We retreat to the mountain and to the safety of our den, our bellies full. Once we arrive, we bathe and take away the essence of our challenging day of fear and satisfaction in the privacy of our home. Then we shall make our beds and get ready to sleep, but we must make sure we are safe, for tomorrow is another day in the life of the snow leopard, a hunter and the hunted.

Rachael Birch (13)
Ellesmere Port Catholic High School, Whitby

Damsel In Distress!

Long ago, there lived a young damsel, Alexandria, who was ruled by her wicked stepmother, Edna. She was locked in a tower on Mount Doom, abandoned from sunlight. For many years she remained up there. There was no way she could escape, she needed help.

Long after, Edna came to say, 'I will hold a tournament, to win your heart. Whoever wins will marry you, but then you must leave the village.' The damsel agreed.

The tournament was held two days later, but for Alexandria, those two days really dragged.

The day of the tournament arrived, good and evil came to battle. Meanwhile, Alexandria had to remain in the tower until the battle was over.

The battle was two days long and at the end there was a winner. The Prince of Welton Heral. However, a villain, Malfau, tried persuading the damsel into marrying him, although it didn't work.

Alexandria was released from the tower to meet Heral. Sadly, there was a slight problem. Heral had a lethal sword stuck to his side, which could kill anyone he wished to marry. It had to be removed quickly and time was running out. Everybody in the village tried to remove it, but it didn't work.

When it came to the last man, everyone stared at him, because the last man was poor and he was wearing rags. He refused to try, as he said, 'I am poor and I may not touch a prince.'

Heral told the man to try, so he did. He was forever onwards known with glory, as he was the one that removed the lethal sword.

Hayley Stephenson (12)
Ellesmere Port Catholic High School, Whitby

Uther's Quest

Once, a long time ago, there lived the bravest king ever and his name was Uther Pendragon. He had a beautiful wife called Elaine, but also had a nemesis known as Ambrosius Aurelias. He was determined to kill Uther and take Elaine for his wife. In a vain attempt to do this he kidnapped Elaine while she was out on her daily stroll.

Uther was outraged at this news and set out to save his queen. He was nearly at Ambrosius' when he ran into one of his guards, a dragon. Uther fought bravely and, though wounded, he won the battle.

Uther entered the castle and heard faint, distant calls for help. He followed them, hoping that they would take him to his stolen wife. The cries took him to a cave, where he saw his darling wife over a pit of horn-backed dragons, eight-inch long monsters with tails harder than a mace and stronger than anything alive. It could knock you out with one swing of its monstrously powerful tail and feast on your flesh and bones, leaving you nothing more than a pile of dust.

'Let her go, Ambrosius! It's me you want!' Uther called.

'Fine,' came the calm, echoing voice of Ambrosius, 'bring it on!'

The fight was one of the century, it went back and forth, until finally Uther managed to knock Ambrosius into the pit of dragons and that finished him instantly. Uther freed his wife and they made their way back to Camelot.

Callum Eager (12)
Ellesmere Port Catholic High School, Whitby

A Day In The Life Of Lauren Duffey

One day, my friend Sarah and I went to the farm to see our horses, Billy and Locket. It was so shocking when we got there, because *they were gone!* We looked in their stables and they were empty.

We went all around the farm to look for them, but nothing. We asked everyone if they had seen them, but no one had. We were scared.

'What shall we do?' shouted Sarah.

'I think I know where they might be,' I said, 'but it is going to be risky.'

'Just tell me,' said Sarah, 'I'll do anything to get Locket back.'

'And I'll do anything to get Billy back,' I replied. 'Well, I think someone has taken them to the *back field!*'

'*The back field!* Big Boy and Zak will trample all over us!'

'Well, it's worth a try.'

So, off we went, up to the back field. I wondered who had taken them.

We got up to the field and there Billy and Locket were, but being guarded by Big Boy and Zak. We opened the gate and Billy and Locket bombed out. Sarah closed the gate, just before Big Boy and Zak tried to get out. Billy and Locket had cantered off though.

Sarah and I ran to find them. When we got to their stables, they were waiting outside and we could tell they wanted to go in, so in they went and had some delicious food.

Lauren Duffey (12)
Ellesmere Port Catholic High School, Whitby

A Day In The Life Of An Alien In The 23rd Century

Hi! My name is Bliger. If you want to find out what I do in my day and to meet my friends and family, read on.

At 9 o'clock I get up and go on the computer. Then after than I have a bath. So go see my sister, she's across the landing.

'Hi Barb! Tell us what you're doing,' said reporter man.

'I'm doing my green skin massage. Why are you bothering me? Why aren't you pestering Bliger?'

'He's having a bath, Barb.'

'Well, the light is off, so he's finished.'

'Bliger, are you finished?'

'Is that you reporter man? Come in, we're going to meet Bob and Bill.'

'This is Bill and Bob, come to Astro Park.'

'This park is cool. Rocket slides, motorcycle roundabouts. Now on to the burger pool.'

'What's that?'

'It's when you go swimming and go burger eating. So, do you fancy it?'

'Yes, that sounds cool.'

'That was really cool, wasn't it reporter man? Let's go home and see Mum.'

At home.

'This is my mum, Bindo.'

'Hi, do you want to make me some tea?'

'Yes, I'll make alien pie. Do you want that Mum, along with pumpkin apple drink?'

'Yes, sounds good.'

'I'll get making then.'

'That was delicious, thanks Bliger.'

'Here's your pudding Mum, alien custard. We're going to see Dad. See you later, Mum!'

'Here's my dad, Bill. He's a mechanic.'

'Sorry Bliger, go and play with robodog, I'm too busy now.'

'Hi robodog, let's play.'

'Well, night everyone. It's been good today. Thanks for hanging out with me!'

Charlotte Dowdall (11)
Ellesmere Port Catholic High School, Whitby

A Day In The Life Of My Nan As A Child

One day Laura came, very excited about her history lesson she was doing about the war. It was her favourite subject. Laura asked her Nan to tell her all about it, what it felt like and how it was. Laura's Nan began . . .

'It was 1939 just before the war started and I was packing my things to leave. My father had to go to fight in the war, it was very sad leaving, because I loved him so much, I went on a boat to America. It was a very tiring journey.

As I was starting to unpack, the sirens went off and they were extremely loud. I was told to take cover. The whole hotel was shaking, it was very frightening. Then the bombs started to drop. It was like thunder, but over a thousand times louder. It was very scary.

As soon as they all stopped. I looked out of the window and all the buildings were demolished and there were dead bodies everywhere. It was the scariest day ever.

As I was about to go to bed, my mother rang, but seemed very upset. She was crying on the phone, so I asked her what was wrong and she said, 'I'm very sorry, but your father has died.'

I started to shake and shiver, my eyes started to sting with pain. I dropped the phone and ran to my room and started to cry. That was the scariest day ever, when the person I loved the most, died and I was ever so young.'

Laura went into school and got an A on her history homework.

Chelsea Bailey (12)
Ellesmere Port Catholic High School, Whitby

A Day In The Life Of Someone Lonely

High was the sky above Victoria Mount, bats were whizzing and whirling around the deserted house of Master Colin Dublin.

We'd all heard in school last Monday, that his beautiful wife Maria, had died. Some people said she had killed herself, others said she was killed. My point of view was, well, I don't really know, but that all changed when I was dared by the evil Harley Martin to go and find out the truth . . .

It was Wednesday night and my mum was watching Countdown, as she always did. (She's so boring!) Anyway, I waited for the break to finish and then I packed a torch, my brother's phone and my closest possession, Tedd. I then slid down the slimy, wet drainpipe, to make a run down to Liam's house, he was coming too.

We walked along the empty streets of Windsor City, with no person or animal in sight.

We then climbed the long, winding mountain to reach Master Colin's house, when we found it empty. Then above the wreath of flowers, laid a note saying, 'In great memory of the Colins family'. After that, we were spooked and ran straight back down towards the town.

Later that week, we found out that it wasn't just Master Colin's wife who had died, it was the rest of them, away from home, visiting another town.

Everyone in school was really disappointed in themselves, because of all the rumours they had started and spread.

Stephanie Atherton (11)
Ellesmere Port Catholic High School, Whitby

Silently Sealed

Days seem longer now. Ever since that tragic day, I've never wanted to look back. I feel trapped inside my own body and it's not right to feel that way.

Although I am better off than half of the people who live in this world, I can't help but wonder whether it's all happened to me on purpose, or have I just been chosen out of many? Either way, it did. And there's no turning back.

The happiness is out of my reach now and it will never move closer (as far as I can look into the future, that is).

My lips have been sealed for a very long time. In fact, ever since it happened. My emotions have been tied and bottled up inside and now it's time to let them out, to whoever is my audience. Only as long as you can keep a secret.

Raising his incredibly large hand, he pushed the air from the side of my face and . . .

A bruise suddenly appeared. A spacious area around my eye was replaced by a dark, murky patch.

I just stood there. I couldn't speak. Nor could I move. My eyes felt hypnotised, as they fell beneath my eyelids. I lost my focus as the world slipped through my fingers. Tears streamed down my face. *Ssh!*

Rebecca Marshall (12)
Fairfield High School for Girls, Droylsden

Her House!

I was going to a friend's house and staying this Friday. I couldn't wait. It got to Friday, I was so excited! When I got to my friend's house, it was not what I had expected. It was different in a way, the way it was laid out.

I went into the living room and there were holes in the sofa and the wallpaper was falling off the walls. The house was horrible and I had to stay overnight. So I thought I would ask for a drink, so we went into the kitchen and it was worse. There were loads of dishes that needed cleaning and the tiles were falling off the wall, so I changed my mind and said no to the drink after all.

We went up into her bedroom because she was always so tidy at school. We got up the stairs and her door was pink and looked clean. I walked in and *argh!* It was horrible and the room was very cheesy; in one corner there was a bed that looked as if it had not been cleaned for ages. There were wardrobes in the other corner and the doors were falling off. Inside there was a load of dirty clothes. The wallpaper was hanging off the wall here too and in the last corner there was a loaded shotgun . . .

Samantha Molloy (12)
Fairfield High School for Girls, Droylsden

Coping Without Them

It was the most upsetting day of my life. School is always so dreary and this day was no exception. When I arrived home, the news I was about to receive was to change my life forever. Gran was sat weeping on my sofa.

'Gran? What's wrong? Where are Mum and Dad?'
'Haven't you heard?' she snivelled.
'Heard what?' I questioned.
'This is hard to tell you, Claire. Your mum and dad died today. In a car crash. I'm so sorry.' She burst into tears.

My heart sank and I fell silent. I would not and could not believe my ears. I raced upstairs and cried for an eternity.

That night, I had calls from neighbours, classmates and family friends, all offering condolences. I just wanted to be left alone. No one understood. The hardest part of it all, was the knowledge that the funeral was still to come.

The service was beautiful, they would have been so proud of the family, yet as it drew to an end, I knew I had to continue life without them. I knew I had to cope . . . somehow.

Hannah Brown (12)
Fairfield High School for Girls, Droylsden

Trapped!

My toes dangled excitedly into the calm water, as the sun beat down onto my back. Listening to all of the happy children, I thought how fantastic it was to be on a school holiday! The row I had had with my sister that morning seemed to be a million miles away.

As I dug my feet into the cold sand, I became aware of a distant whispering. At first I paid no attention. Minutes passed, until I heard the sound again. My eyes were drawn in the direction of the strange noises, whereupon I saw a small entrance to a gloomy cave.

Leaning forward, my ears strained as the whispering became a name, 'Sophie.' Cautiously, I ambled over, hoping to see a friendly face appear, that was when I felt the cool ocean lapping against my ankles. I spun round and to my horror, I saw that the beach had been replaced by the incoming tide. There was no escape but to go into the underground prison.

Anxiously, my eyes struggled to become accustomed to the dark. I felt petrified and alone, apart from the voices coming from all around. Panicking, I stumbled on, not sure of my direction. Grasping tight onto the wall, I could feel the dampness and slime oozing through my fingers. The row I had had with my sister didn't seem so bad. Conscious that the sea was now at my knees, I wasn't sure whether I'd see daylight again! Was I to survive . . . ?

Sophia Austin (12)
Fairfield High School for Girls, Droylsden

The Woman

Sergeant Jemma sat back in her chair. This was going to be a long day. She had already had a nosy neighbour reporting a fight in a back garden. Suddenly, the phone rang. Jemma picked up the receiver. A worried, old woman babbled something down the phone. She sounded very shaken. 'Where are you?' Jemma asked, trying to sound reassuring.

'1 J-J-Jumb-b-ble Road,' she stammered.

'I'll be there in ten minutes,' sighed Jemma, as she put the receiver down.

A horrible sight awaited Jemma at the house. A young, beautiful woman was dangling by her neck from the loft window of 1 Jumble Road. The old woman had passed out on the unkempt lawn.

The forensics searched the area, but could find no clues. The woman's death was a complete mystery. The only thing they knew was her name, Malory Blackthorn. A few months later and the case had been abandoned. It was put down as suicide.

Jemma was walking her dog along the canal. A woman with a big, black hat bent down to stroke Scooby. Jemma realised with a start that the woman was Malory! Her heart stopped.

After having tea and biscuits with the 'ghost' of Malory, Jemma understood. Malory was still dead, this was her twin sister, Margrat. She had the answers to the death. She told Jemma all about the way she had murdered Malory, before she murdered Jemma too.

Katherine Barr (12)
Fairfield High School for Girls, Droylsden

A New House

The clouds are black, the rain is dull. That is what it is like at our new house, it is an old house, with red bricks which are covered in moss. I'm inside. The rooms are massive and covered in cream and the kitchen is overlooking a patch of lawn and a dingy shed, where the door is hanging off. But I do suppose that it matches the street name which is Wood Avenue . . .

'Tom, come here. Come and help me unpack this box, it is so heavy because it's got that stereo in it,' came the sound of his mother from the pick up truck.

'Alright Mum, but can I go out after?' said Tom.

'Of course you can, but make sure you're back for 8 o'clock.'

So, off Tom went. When he got to the park, there were lots of little gangs all in huddles and sniggering to each other about what programme they had watched the night before. He stood in awe, when all of a sudden, a ball flew into his face. He stood there and then kicked the ball back.

After that, he noticed something shiny, so he went over and found what looked like a watch, but with lots of buttons. He pressed one, *big mistake!*

Tom got warped off and found himself in a cold and blue world, where there were crab creatures walking around. All of a sudden, they rushed for him. Tom kept pressing his buttons and finally got back to his house, in his own bedroom!

Samantha Wilbraham (12)
Fairfield High School for Girls, Droylsden

Mini Saga

I stepped out in front of the car. It was time to go. I felt the blood rush to my head. I heard a distant voice calling me, it got louder and louder. The anticipation was intense.

'Come on, you have to go to the dentist!'

I got into the car.

Sarah McGuire (12)
Fairfield High School for Girls, Droylsden

I'm A Kid, Get Me Out Of Here

We drove past a really old, creepy house on the way to our hotel. To our surprise, the hotel was next door!

The day after, my brother Josh and I were allowed to go off on our own. We went to the pool bar to get a drink of Fanta and an ice lolly. In the corner we spotted a boy and a girl. We went over to them. The girl had long, blonde hair, the boy was thin and also had blond hair.

Josh asked the boy his name and I asked the girl. The boy replied Sam and the girl replied Chloe.

Josh had a bright idea! He said, 'Why don't we go and explore the spooky house?' We all agreed. We all walked to the house which hadn't been lived in for forty years!

We went into the house. First we explored the cellar. It was cold and full of cobwebs! Then we went upstairs. The first thing we came to was just a plain, old bathroom, with a bath, toilet and sink.

The next room we came to was very creepy. Chloe and I did not go in, but Sam and Josh did! The door slammed shut behind them. It was hiding the dreadful secret!

The next thing we heard was, 'I'm a kid, get me out of here!'

Sally Devine (12)
Kingswood College, Scarisbrick

A Day In The Life Of Stripes, My Rabbit

Great, ants have made a home again in my house, or as my owner puts it, 'That stinky hutch!' I've been waiting now for an hour to be let out to roam the back garden and go and see my friend, Peter the robin.

There she is, moaning that she had to get up early, even though she had breakfast and I have had to wait to get mine.

Great, it's the food that looks like hamster food. Oh well, as they say, eat what you get.

Oh no, the cat's back. Better sit really still, but this buzzing bee is making me twitch. He keeps landing on my nose.

What I would do to be in that warm house, instead of in this back garden. I suppose though, it's nice to lounge in the sun, always doing nothing else but eating and watching butterflies flutter about in the summer breeze. It's really fun though, at night-time when it's dark and the bright moon is out.

The moan monster is back, to put me away, but forgets to fill up my water bottle. So, because of this, I run up one end of the garden away from her and then run in-between her legs and into the bush. After about 20 minutes of exercise, I calmly walk into my hutch and realise, the ants have gone.

As the owl hoots, I slowly drift off into a lovely state of slumber.

Goodnight!

Jayne Bode (14)
Kingswood College, Scarisbrick

A Day In The Life Of A Nobody

My day starts OK. Get up, go to school, but once I get there, up to form period, my day really starts. I get shoved around and no one helps me up when I fall over and people tramp by. Sometimes they even tramp over me.

I get to first class and sit in my usual place, middle desk, front row. A cruel voice asks me why teacher's pet is not in a cage? I hate that phrase. I am not teacher's pet; I just work hard - unlike some people.

I carry on like this throughout the day. Working hard, with my head down. Bits of rubber and pieces of rolled-up paper get thrown at me, when no one is looking.

The day passes quickly, but not quickly enough. My locker gets kicked in and someone steals my lunch. A usual day.

As I walk past the train station, on my way home, a man walks into me and doesn't even notice. Am I a ghost? I feel like one. A ghost trapped in amongst people who don't want me, or care about me. I like that thought - if I am a ghost, then no one can ever hurt me again. I smile to myself, happy at last.

Catriona Walker (13)
Kingswood College, Scarisbrick

Hotel California

Monica wasn't happy with her assignment. She was sure her boss had only sent her to the hotel to keep her out of the newsroom. Once in her room, Monica flopped down on top of the bed. There was a knock on the door, an old-fashioned maid handed over some linen without a word and left. *Strange*, thought Monica.

Monica slipped between the cool sheets and tried to sleep, but at 2.30am she woke, hot and sweaty. Opening her eyes, she gasped as she saw the maid sitting opposite her bed. She reached out to touch the woman, she was icy cold! Monica jumped back in fright! The sight of the cold body was too much and Monica fainted. It wasn't just the feel of the body that had given her such a fright, it was the face! She recognised the face as that of her great grandmother, Elizabeth.

'Elizabeth?' whispered Monica.

'What do you know of Elizabeth?' spluttered the woman.

Monica explained that her great grandmother, Elizabeth, had died of fever in this very hotel.

'Elizabeth did indeed die in this hotel, she was murdered! A sleeping potion was put in her warm milk, then while she was dozing, he stabbed her 19 times. No one ever discovered who had done it, although some suspected the manager, Mr Boocockly!'

Monica closed her eyes, trying to take in what she had just been told. When she opened her eyes, the woman had gone!

Dressing quickly, Monica rushed downstairs and was ushered into the manager's office. She told her story whilst the manager listened intently. Then there was an icy silence in the room.

'That was an interesting story,' said the man slowly, 'but rather far-fetched I think, don't you?'

Monica was annoyed. 'Who are you anyway?' she asked.

'My name's Mr Boocockly, the great grandson of the original manager, that you have just accused of murder.'

Monica, struggling to catch her breath, staggered to her feet. 'I'm a journalist!' she shouted. 'I'm going to make sure this story makes the headlines at last!'

In her room, she typed until she was exhausted. At 1.00am there was a knock on the door. There was the maid, with a welcoming cup of hot milk, just what Monica needed to help her sleep.

She settled back in her chair, slowly sipping the warm milk. Her eyes felt tired. She felt herself drifting off to sleep . . .

Later that night, a shadow crept across the wall of Monica's room. The floorboards creaked, before a blood-curdling scream of terror was heard throughout the hotel . . .

Emily Thorley (12)
Montgomery High School, Blackpool

Innocent Till Proven Guilty

One night I was driving home from work, when I came to a sudden halt. I sat there, shocked, then decided to get out. It was dark. The moon was overcast by clouds, whilst the gloomy lamplight flickered constantly in the almost overpoweringly black night sky.

Underneath the car wheels was a young, pale child. The road was bloodstained, the boy lay motionless and the wind rustled the nearby trees. I moved closer and touched his ghostly, white face. It was ice-cold to the touch, even through my thick woollen gloves, as if he'd been there for hours. I thought that surely only a few minutes into the accident he would still be breathing, but he was dead.

I slid slowly back into the car and drove around for the whole night, feeling guilty.

Finally I decided to go back home, my husband was waiting. He started an argument, accusing me of having an affair. I swore that I hadn't, but he just would not believe me. That's when I stormed out, leapt back into my car and drove off. I intended to drive past the place that I'd left the boy.

A policeman stopped me. By now tears were streaming down my face, I opened the window and blurted out the whole story.

'Now I'm here, sitting at this desk, telling you my story.'

'Well, I'm going to have to let you go, Ma'am. I mean, it's obvious you didn't kill him.'

Chelsey Lowenna Clarke (13)
Montgomery High School, Blackpool

You're Nicked!

They hadn't had an argument for as long as they had been together, but Gregg knew that this time he had to put his foot down.

Sheena, his wife, had only been away for a few hours, but he couldn't help feeling guilty when the police car pulled up outside the house on the London street. The tall policeman stepped into the house, holding a pen in one hand and a pad in the other, which displayed the Metropolitan Police badge. He stepped in quietly and told Gregg that he had better sit down.

Gregg was horrified at the news of his wife's death, she had been involved in a fatal road accident. He was even more shocked however, when he was told that he was being held responsible, as all the clues added up to him being the culprit. The policeman escorted him to the waiting car, then it left the street.

Gregg received five years in prison.

Gregg sat on the bed in his cell, staring at his tired face in the mirror, above the washbasin. He stood up and walked up and down his cell. He approached the window on the far wall, then leant against it, staring at the surrounding grounds of the prison and the tall, black gates. There was a sudden clatter as they were pulled open slowly and in drove a dark blue car.

It pulled up outside the main doors and a blonde woman slid out. She seemed so familiar to Gregg. She leant against the car, staring at the main doors, they opened with a *click*.

Out of the door came the officer that had arrested Gregg. He approached the woman, wrapped his arms around her, then kissed her.

'Sheena!' cried Gregg, as she quickly entered the car.

Charlotte Darlington (13)
Montgomery High School, Blackpool

But . . . ?

David loved his fiancée very much. It had destroyed him when she'd disappeared three months ago. Since then, he had had a tumour in his brain and with this came the fits.

One night, he sat in his lounge looking at Lucinda's photograph. He threw it across the room! 'Why did you go Luce?'

He took a deep drag on his cigarette and exhaled heavily, looking at the heap of smashed glass. 'What did I do that was so bad you had to go?'

Next door, Doris had heard. She rang the mental institution.

David's doorbell rang at 8.00am. He rose from his settee, where he'd fallen asleep. He glanced at the smashed frame, 'God! What've I done?' He went to the front door.

'Hello, David?'
'Yes?'
'We've had a report of you having fits.'
'What?' David was surprised. 'Who said that?'
'Sorry, we don't give out names.'
'So, what are you doing?'
'Sorry, we are going to have to take you away.'

David started running away, but two other men came out of the back of a van. They grabbed him and put him in the back of the van.

When they got there, the two men carried David into a room with no windows or shelves, nothing. Just an old bed. The door was metal. There was no escape.

David lived there for three years.

David walked out into the fresh air. He was free. He got a taxi to his local.

'A pint please, love.'
'OK,' the barmaid replied.
David recognised the voice from somewhere. He looked up.
'Lucinda?'
'David!'
'Lucinda!'

He leant forward to hug her, but she backed away. A man walked up to Lucinda and kissed her.

David looked at Lucinda's finger. She had on an engagement ring, but it wasn't his!

Emily Taylor (12)
Montgomery High School, Blackpool

Depression

I sat in the cold, dark school classroom, which had once been mine. As a child I knew teaching was the ambition most suited to me. I had my dream job, my life could not have been made any better. Until that day, it was so out of character. Every day I ask myself over and over, 'Why, why did you lash out? You had everything you ever dreamt of and more.'

It was a Monday morning, I've never really understood why so many people dislike Monday mornings, for me, Monday mornings are the best of them all.

I strolled into my classroom without a care in the world and greeted my new class with a smile.

Unfortunately, my new class was the class from Hell! They were awful; running, screaming, swearing and generally just doing what they pleased. As the day was growing older, I began to lose my patience with one boy in particular.

David Parker! He had been shouting awful abuse at me all day and I just couldn't take it for a second more. I lashed out. I hit the poor child. I simply cannot imagine what had been going through my head at the time.

I felt so awful afterwards. I confessed all to the head teacher and the police. All of this happened exactly a year ago to this day. Today is my first day of freedom and I chose to come back to this place, the place where all my finest fulfilled hopes and dreams remain.

Isn't it funny how life has a way of taking everything you think to be of importance to you, just when you're at your highest point?

Sally Halliwell (12)
Montgomery High School, Blackpool

Grandfather

It was a cold, damp Saturday morning. I knew it was going to be one of those days. My brother and sister were arguing and Mum and Dad were already well into the first argument of the day.

The phone rang, it was Sally. We were meant to be going into town. I was looking forward to getting out of this mad house, but Sally had rung to cancel. I couldn't stand staying any longer. I was starting to get a headache and my stomach was rumbling. There would be no chance of getting any breakfast, as the argument between Mum and Dad was just about to get ten times worse, so I decided to go to the café round the corner.

It wasn't far, but by the time I got there, I was soaking wet. It was empty, so I ordered a plate of chips, a drink of tea and sat down next to a man, old aged, about 60-70 I would have guessed, and he was unusually pale. He looked up at me and smiled, he looked sort of familiar, but I couldn't quite figure out where I had seen him before.

We started chatting, I told him about the trouble at home, I don't know why, it had nothing to do with him, it was family business, but I felt as if I could talk to him.

I was surprised at the amount of advice he gave me. It was as if he knew all about the situation, before I had even told him.

We got up and left. He walked me home, but before I had a chance to say thank you and goodbye, he had gone.

I opened the door expecting to be deafened by the noise, but it was surprisingly quiet. I went up to my bedroom and closed the door. Soon after, all hell broke loose again. I put my headphones on, music full blast and lay on my bed. I reached up onto the shelf, next to my bedside table and grabbed the first book I touched.

It was an old album, mostly containing pictures of old parties, Christmas, holidays etc. I turned over to the last page and there was a picture of Mum and the man I had sat with in the café, I was sure of it.

I ran downstairs and flung the picture in her face. We never spoke about past relatives, great uncles, aunts and so on. I nearly collapsed when she told me who he was. It was my grandfather, who had died of a heart attack years before I was born.

Chelsey Cross (13)
Montgomery High School, Blackpool

The Most Gullible Person In The World

Barry (Baz for short) was the most gullible person in the world. If anything was asked of him, he'd do it, he wouldn't want to, but he'd do it. One time, in Year 4, Billy Wilson dared Baz (he'd like to use the word asked) to shoot a hare with a pellet gun. This was especially hard for Baz, because he was a vegetarian, but he'd been asked to do something and he felt is was his duty to do it. He took hold of the gun, with his sweaty, shaking hands and . . . *bang!*

It was the Chicago County Fair and Baz was ready for anything his 'friends' were going to 'ask' him. First, he was asked to go on the 'coaster with Joey. He agreed and strapped himself in. He was going higher and higher and then noticed that Joey was not by his side. He was scared. In front of him stood 72 feet of track, three loops and four drops at a speed of 51mph.

After the three minutes of hell, Baz went to the nearest bin, tried to aim his head and vomited all over it. After that ride, he'd had enough and was down to his last 25 cents. Out of the corner of his eye, he saw a wish machine that only cost 2 cents. He put the coin in and shouted, 'I . . . I wish I wasn't so gullible!'

A card came out of the machine that read, 'Your wish has been granted'. Baz smiled faintly and went home.

The next morning, Baz walked to school, because the water level was too high to go on his skateboard. His first lesson was maths. As he got to his room, he saw Joey bounding at him with a pile of books. Baz knew what he was going to ask and he was *sure* that he'd say, 'No!'

Joseph Packman (13)
Montgomery High School, Blackpool

Cats

Thirty-year-old Janet lived alone with two dogs. She hated cats, as they frequently attacked the birds in her garden.

It had just turned 8 o'clock on a Tuesday morning and as usual, she was late! Once she had jumped out of bed and put on her clothes, she looked in the mirror. She gazed at herself in amazement, as she had turned into a cat!

Janet had decided to make the most of it. In her back garden, she had already run away from her two dogs, but now she had seen a nearby bird.

Prowling up to the bird on the lawn, Janet pounced, like a leopard, onto the bird. Soon it was in her mouth.

After ten minutes of playing with it, she had actually killed the poor thing! The bird lay there, all crumpled and dripping with blood from where her teeth marks had pierced holes.

Janet prowled around the garden, looking for something to eat. She managed to find some bread that had been put out for the birds the other day.

Still trying to forget about the bird she had earlier savagely killed, she realised that it wasn't the cats' fault what they were doing to the birds, even though they knew what they were doing, she realised it was only their natural instinct.

Soon it became dark outside, so she decided to go through the dog flap in her back door. Once she had leapt onto her chair, she soon fell asleep, hoping the day had just been a dream.

Andrea Norton (12)
Montgomery High School, Blackpool

Your Dream, My Nightmare

'This is the most boring story I've ever read!' remarked Willow, rudely.

'Thank you. I really wanted my best friend to say that about my life-long dream!' replied Rina, close to tears.

'Willow, time to go!' her mother called.

As Willow arrived, the street plunged into darkness.

'Oh no,' groaned her mother.

At last, Willow collapsed onto her bed, feeling very tired.

She couldn't see, it was dark. Taking a step forward, her foot hit a wall. Squinting hard, she saw a well, leaning in for a better look, she panicked as she lost her balance. She fell.

It was cold, dark and wet. Willow remembered landing when she had woken, her head felt like it was split with the pain. The water around her was freezing. She couldn't stop shivering. She had to get out. The walls were uneven, perhaps she could climb, but the walls were also slippy and dangerous.

She was almost at the top, groping blindly for a handhold when suddenly, her fingers exploded with pain. She was falling again.

The floor she smashed upon, was not the well's, but that of her bedroom. Rina's story wasn't so boring after all.

Willow ran downstairs to phone Rina, she hit her fingers on the door, which hurt more than it should have.

'Your face!' gasped her mother, wide-eyed in shock.

Willow looked in the mirror, she looked like a leopard. Her whole body was covered in bruises and her fingers were caked in blood, from where her nails had been ripped off.

Amanda Jones (12)
Montgomery High School, Blackpool

Drugs

Jim walked down the deserted alley with his mates. No street lights were visible. An ideal place for a drug gang. It was their usual meeting place and Jim had told his mum that he was going to the cinema with Fred, another drug taker. There were four of them altogether. Jim, Fred, Bob and Adam. Adam was the one who acquired the drugs; the rest smoked or sniffed them. Jim revealed his cash, that was supposedly his cinema money and gave it to Adam. He took the money from him and put it in his back pocket.

The gang all took in a deep breath of cannabis and blew it out. '*Mmmmm,*' everyone said.

They had been taking cannabis since they were 14. They were now 15 or 16. Jim was 16, Fred was 15, Bob was 15 and Adam was 16.

Jim and Fred coughed. Adam had also sneaked out some Febreze to get the smell out of all their clothes.

All of a sudden, Jim fainted, banging his head against the corner of the wall. He didn't get up. Adam had only one choice. To phone the emergency services.

'Can I have an ambulance please? My friend has banged his head and he isn't moving.'

'What was he doing?'

'Smoking.'

'OK. Where are you?'

'Trindle Way, Penrith.'

'An ambulance is on its way.'

'Thanks,' said Adam and put the phone down.

'Quick guys, finish the cannabis. The ambulance is on its way,' said Fred, getting a bit worried.

They all quickly finished their cannabis and threw the ends over a wall. The ambulance arrived and a man and woman came over with the equipment. They revived him almost straight away and put him in the ambulance. They rang his mum and she met him at the hospital.

'What were you doing, Jim?' asked his mum.

'Smoking cannabis,' said Jim, beginning to cry.

'Oh dear,' said his mum and fainted.

Michael Scobie (13)
Montgomery High School, Blackpool

I Dare You!

It was a regular weekend, no school, but loads of homework. I wanted to go out, but I couldn't until I'd finished my maths. It was a lovely day and I was stuck inside doing work.

Finally, I'd finished, good timing too. Just then, I heard the doorbell, I ran downstairs and opened the door. It was Gary.

'Alright Rabbit?' he asked.

Rabbit's my nickname. It's because I have big ears and teeth that hang over my bottom lip.

'Comin' out?'

'Yeah, I'll get my shoes!' I replied.

I'm Gary's best mate. Actually, I'm his only mate. No one likes him much. It's because he always wears the same yellow T-shirt and the same blue pants and jacket every day. He never brushes his hair or teeth. It's disgusting, but I'm really clean and I hate dirt and everyone calls me a wuss.

'Hurry up!'

'OK!' I yelled.

We went to an old abandoned bus stop near Gary's house.

'What should we do?' Gary asked.

'Let's go on the roof!' I suggested.

'No!' he replied, firmly.

'Oh . . . sorry . . . heights!'

Gary hates heights, he gets terrified.

'Let's play dares,' I said.

'Yeah, OK!'

'I dare you to climb that scaffolding.' I pointed to a rickety, 50ft high scaffold.

'No way!'

'Chicken!'

'Argh! Fine!'

He started to climb, I followed. It was halfway up when he couldn't go any further. He tried to come back down, but slipped and fell. I heard a thud! I climbed down as fast as I could and he was just stood there! No cuts. No bruises.

'Are you OK?' I asked.

'Yeah.'

'You just fell 25ft!'

'I know.'

'Are you sure you're OK?'

'Yes!'

'OK . . . wait there!'

I ran over to get my bag, when suddenly it was there. A body. A dead body. He was in a yellow T-shirt and blue pants and jacket. It was horrible. It was disgusting. It was . . . Gary!

Emma Hughes (13)
Montgomery High School, Blackpool

A Great Day Out . . .

Rebecca Shaw and Fiona Wilson were going to appear on 'Behind The Door', a quiz show.

They sat in their dressing room. Rebecca was agitated and Fiona was a bit quiet. Fiona was sat on the sexy, black couch, with a dull face.

'You're on,' the executive producer shouted through the door.

Fiona got up slouching and walked, dragging her heavy feet. They made their way to the studio. Fiona started to get dizzy.

'Fi, are you alright?'

'Yeah, fine,' Fiona sighed. She fainted onto the ground.

'Fi! Fi! Ring an ambulance. Quick! She's going to die!'

The executive producer ran down the corridor to ring for an ambulance. 'It will be here in 10 minutes,' the executive producer screamed.

The ambulance arrived and the paramedics rushed towards Fiona. Rebecca sat there, stiff with shock. The paramedics slowly moved her out of the way.

'We are going to have to take her to hospital. She is deteriorating fast!' the young paramedic tried to say calmly. The paramedics wheeled Fiona into the ambulance and Rebecca followed.

Rebecca shook as the ambulance jolted around corners. All the time they were in the ambulance, Rebecca held Fiona's hand and begged that she wasn't going to die.

When they got to the hospital, Fiona was rushed into the Accident and Emergency department. An anxious Rebecca waited for news of her best friend. She noticed nurses running to help her friend. She watched as the doctors turned the monitors off.

'I'm sorry Rebecca. Fiona died of a heroin overdose.'

'Oh my God!'

Hannah Walsh (12)
Montgomery High School, Blackpool

The New House

I was driving down the road to my new house. It was a really sunny day, but the street was completely deserted. Huge houses towered over me. I turned the corner and I saw the smallest house on the street, with a *Sold* sign outside, in the front garden. I pulled up in front of the gate and stepped out of the car.

I walked up to the front door and as I opened it, it made a loud creak, as though it had not been opened in years. I kept walking on. I didn't have any of my things with me, because the removal truck had not arrived yet, so I decided to look around the house.

I started with the room I was in, which was the living room. It was really big, but completely empty. It echoed when I walked.

I heard a noise above me. It was like a big bang. I walked up the stairs slowly and along the landing towards a door at the end. I walked straight on, slowly, towards the door. I put my hand on the handle and tried to open the door, but it was locked. I tried again and to my surprise it opened. I stepped inside.

When I looked around, I saw a woman sitting in a chair. She had shoulder-length blonde hair and very pale skin. She had been reading a book. When she saw me she stood up.

I said, 'Hello. *Erm . . .* what are you doing in my house?'

'Hi. My name is June. How are you?' she answered.

'Fine. What are you doing here?'

'I just bought the house.'

'You can't have! I just bought it.'

When I looked around, I saw in the corner, a pile of what looked like people.

'They're dead!' said June.

Jade Dickinson (12)
Montgomery High School, Blackpool

The All Hallows Mystery

It was a warm summer's evening and it was the fifth anniversary of a murder. Two people thought there was something mysterious about the murder. One of them was Henrietta McGoose. She was ugly and tall. She had ginger hair, with brown eyes, a sloping nose and she was fat. The other teenager was Robert Apple. He was fat and ugly. He had black hair and he was tall too.

They were investigating Henry McGoose's death at All Hallows High School. They searched for clues, then Robert found something.

'Come and have a look over here,' said Robert.

'What is it?' asked Henrietta.

'It's an old, green, sweaty sock.'

'Cool! It could be a clue,' said Henrietta.

Henrietta and Robert took the sock into the school's laboratory to see if it was a lead. The science teacher was in school and tested it for DNA. The science teacher was also in school trying to solve the mystery, so he had some of Henry McGoose's DNA and it matched the sample. They chatted about their discovery on their way home.

'Do you think it could be a lead?' asked Robert.

'Yes. It must be a lead. The DNA matched.'

They then bumped into Mr Paparachi, the school's caretaker.

'Sir, do you know Henry McGoose?' asked Robert.

'Yes, he's my next-door neighbour. Why do you ask?'

'We're investigating his murder.'

'But he's my neighbour.'

'He's my father. How many McGoose's do you know?'

'One.'

'I want to meet him then . . .'

Daniel McKay (12)
Montgomery High School, Blackpool

Holiday From Hell

It was roughly 6.30am on a cold, bitter day. The Johnson family were just about to leave for their skiing holiday in Switzerland. Stacey was really excited, as this would be her first time skiing.

'Mum, taxi's here,' shouted Stacey, as the taxi pulled up.

Sophie was 37, had a good job and enjoyed skiing regularly in France, but never before in Switzerland.

'Hurry up, Bill!' she said, whilst taking the suitcases to the taxi.

Bill came running down the stairs and locked the front door.

'Where to?' asked the taxi driver.

'Airport please,' replied Bill, excitedly.

The taxi drive was long and boring. Stacey had eventually fallen asleep, but no one else could because of the taxi's roaring engine. They pulled up at the airport, knowing they had an eight-hour flight ahead of them.

Luckily for them, the plane was on time and they got straight on board. The plane seemed unusually cold, but everybody just ignored it and sat down.

The jet engines started and the whirling sound filled the plane as it roared into action. The speed was amazing and the plane glided into the air.

It was about 30 minutes into the journey when the engine on the right wing caught fire and the plane started to plummet towards the sea.

'This is the captain speaking, please will everybody take out their lifebelts as we prepare for evacuation.'

There was screaming coming from all directions, as one by one everybody jumped out of the plane.

Stacey jumped out of the plane just as it whirled into the cliffs with an ear-piercing bang!

Most of the other passengers died, but Stacey and Sophie managed to scramble onto the cliffs. Bill had died and they later got rescued by a passing P&O ferry.

Stephen Middleton (13)
Montgomery High School, Blackpool

Football Injury

Dan was playing football. His friend whipped in an amazing cross, aimed at the far post. Dan was running in to head the ball. The keeper had been wrong-footed and watched as the ball floated over his head. Dan jumped and headed the ball, which went flying into the goal, but *crack*, he had collided with the post. Dan crashed to the ground.

Dan was only 14, but he had been injured more times than most people have in their whole lives. He had broken his left ankle twice and his right ankle once. He had broken his collarbone twice and his left arm three times and now he was in hospital again.

He opened his right eye, but he couldn't open his left one because it was swollen. He turned his head and his mum and dad jumped forward and hugged him. Suddenly, he fell back and fainted.

Dan suddenly woke up, he must have been having a bad dream. He looked at the clock, it was three in the afternoon. His parents weren't there and nobody had noticed that he had woken up. Dan also noticed that it was very dark in the room he was in. He got up and walked out of the room. No one noticed him. He walked home and opened the door. He sat next to his mum and she still didn't see him, but he saw that she was crying. He picked up the paper that was on the table and read the front page. It said: 'Child, aged 14, dies in hospital'.

It also had a picture of Dan.

Jamie Salter (13)
Montgomery High School, Blackpool

Chicken!

Here I am, Dave Haddock, stood on the 'Wall of Doom', facing the biggest task of my life. I had gained the title 'King of Stunts', I'm on a fifty foot wall ready to jump. I hear my public chanting, 'Chicken!' I'm standing and a question keeps running through my mind, *how did I get here?* The same flashback of the week's events comes back . . .

'Dave, the stunts are running dry, there's a rumour going round that you're going to lose your title unless you do something soon.'

I hear Billy retorting as we walk down the miserable corridor, Billy is still yakking on.

'A guy just jumped from a 20ft tree. The rumour is that he is going to take your title. The only way you can beat that is to jump off the 'Wall of Doom' and you've got to be stupid to do that.' Billy, a short boy with mousy hair, is lecturing me when he has only ever received a swimming award.

'I can jump that any day!' I recall myself saying . . .

That's how I got to where I am now. It's a good job I'm so high, so that my public cannot see the yellow stain growing on my trousers.

'Chicken! Chicken!' The chant is getting louder. It's now or never. Here goes . . .

I pull myself up from the ground, I slowly glance upwards, I listen for the applause, but all I hear is sobs. I see a graze on my knee and I stand and shout, 'What's wrong?' No one answers me.

I walk through the streets pondering over what happened. I wave at the butcher, but he just stares. I see an ambulance rushing down the street. A boy is led, motionless, on a stretcher and that's when I realise . . .

Linzi Hull (12)
Montgomery High School, Blackpool

Eyes Of A Sea Dragon

Except for being a little homesick, Sarah was having the time of her life. The adventuresome thirteen-year-old had arrived at the home of her uncle Max and cousin Megan, who lived in the outskirts of Glenwick, Scotland. Sarah was spending the next two weeks with them, whilst her parents enjoyed their second honeymoon in France.

'Tell me more about the Loch Ness Monster,' she urged her cousin, as they hiked the path down to the loch where the creature was supposed to have been sighted.

'I read that some people think it's some kind of giant eel,' Sarah explained, stepping over a huge rock in her path and leaping onto a dry patch of green land.

Megan chuckled and tossed her red curls over her shoulders. 'Yes and some people think that Nessie is a huge worm-like dinosaur left over from the prehistoric times. I just think that the whole thing is a stupid, silly myth,' Megan exclaimed, making a funny face. Her freckle-sprinkled nose scrunched up and her hand tucked her blowing curls behind her shoulder once more.

'I've heard that people have actually caught pictures of the monster,' Sarah answered, tugging her limp, brown hair thoughtfully, whilst staring at her cousin's curls enviously.

Megan rolled her blue eyes. 'Fake. People who claim to have caught Nessie on camera, video and anything else, are only looking for money. Trust me. They're all phonies.'

'You're probably right,' Sarah replied, a note of disappointment in her voice, as she followed her freckle-faced cousin towards the loch.

'Well, there it is. The most famous lake worldwide, Loch Ness,' Megan answered.

The lake came into view and Megan stopped and pointed to the desolate grey water surrounded by a light mist. The blue sky beamed down onto the lake's surface making it glimmer. A small, brown, freckled bird swooped down and skimmed the water gently and gracefully with one wing. A slight, warm breeze ran its hand across the girls' faces as they stared. The mountains rose high and proud behind the dazzling water, like kings on thrones.

'It's beautiful. Can we get a little closer to the water?' asked Sarah, raising her silver camera and angling it as she shot numerous photos.

Megan nodded woodenly and started to walk towards the loch. 'No serpent,' Megan teased, looking at her cousin.

Together Megan and Sarah walked along the sandy shore towards a huge cluster of big boulders a few kilometres away. Sarah watched her cousin settle on one of the boulders and looked beyond. Suddenly, she felt her hair on the back of her neck stand on end. Her mouth fell open and her trembling finger pointed at the object causing her to freeze. Megan spun around at the direction her cousin pointed at.

'I don't believe it,' she screamed, her face turning white. 'It's not possible!'

The two girls slowly approached a huge, reptilian creature lying half on the shore and half in the icy water of the loch. It had to be at least 12 metres in length and looked as though it weighed about 5-10 tonnes. It had scales which appeared dry and rough in the sun.

Sarah scanned the creature slowly with her wide, green eyes. A long, scrawny neck lay limply on the sand and a huge, pale green stomach could be seen along with four, majestic, leathery-looking flippers, two on each side of the body. *Turtle flippers*, Megan thought.

'Is it the monster?' stuttered Megan, all of her freckles now completely invisible.

'It has to be! Just look at the size of it! It's Nessie all right!' gasped Sarah. A sad look suddenly came over her face. 'Doesn't it look sick, kind of helpless in a way?'

She advanced towards the serpent and slowly bent down until her denim knees touched the sand comfortably.

Megan cried out, 'Don't go near!' She trembled, but made no effort to pull her cousin back.

'The poor thing's beached itself,' commented Sarah.

'Sick whales do it, so why not a sick sea monster?' answered Megan, feeling her fear decrease.

The two girls looked on at the still creature in utter silence for many minutes, not knowing what to do or to expect. Sarah reached forward and touched the serpent's scaly head with her left hand. She shot back in shock.

'Yuck!' she squealed. 'It feels like . . . rubber!'

Megan stared silently at the creature's statue, frozen body and then glanced at her cousin.

Growing braver, Sarah trailed her hand along the creature's cheek and down its neck and stopped when her fingers found three long slits of its gills. She froze and went cold. There was warm air exhaling from the gills. 'It's alive!' she cried out in alarm, as she raced over to her cousin.

Clutching each other, the two girls scrambled away from the beast and stared at its mouth, now slowly opening, to expose rows and rows of curved, oversized fangs. A black, forked tongue flickered through the fangs as a deep, gurgling hiss escaped from the reviving beast whose eyes slowly opened and fixed on the two trembling girls.

'Look at the eyes!' gasped Sarah, clinging tighter to Megan.

'They're . . . like . . . intelligent! Almost human-like eyes!' She gasped in amazement as the monster raised its head slightly from the shore. The monster stared at them pleadingly, before dropping its head limply onto the sand once more.

'Let's get my dad. He'll know what to do,' whispered Megan, in Sarah's left ear.

Sarah nodded and released her cousin and slowly stood up. The monster looked at them again, its eyes filled with sorrow and despair.

'We'll be back, I promise,' Sarah murmured gently. She walked towards Nessie, very gently and reached out her trembling hand. Megan looked on, as her cousin stroked the rubbery cheek of the dying sea monster. Sarah moved away from the monster and took her cousin's hand and together they raced back to the house.

Five years ago, Megan's father had suffered a spinal injury in a car crash and was now mostly confined to a wheelchair, however, he did manage to get around with crutches and leg braces when he needed to. When he heard Sarah and Megan's story, he was determined that nothing would keep him from seeing the fabled creature.

Slowly and with considerable difficulty, he followed the girls down to the lake on his crutches. When they finally reached the site where the creature lay, their hearts sank. Totally limp now, her head and long, tapering neck were draped on shore, half submerged in the lapping water. Her eyes were closed and she looked weaker than ever. Sarah walked up to it carefully and bent down onto her knees. Max clutched Megan to his chest, as he watched Sarah's chest start to heave.

'She's dying,' she sobbed. She covered her face with her hands and forced herself not to look at the dying creature. The scales were no longer pale green, but now they were pure grey. Its chest gasped for air and deep, rasping gurgles came from its throat. Sarah reached forward with her left hand and placed it onto one of the three gills. It wasn't breathing. 'No! Please no!' she wailed, tears streaking down her cheeks, she held the tip of one of the flippers.

Megan burst into tears and wrapped her arms around her father.

'There's nothing we can do. I'm sorry,' he whispered to Sarah and Megan.

'No!' yelled Sarah, wiping tears from her face. 'She can't be dead! I promised we'd be back for her!' Tears fell from her eyes onto the creature's chest and face. She felt her cousin's hand on her shoulder.

She allowed her cousin to drag her away from the dead creature and sobbed, sadly.

As they turned away, they heard a sudden ruffle of sand behind them.

'It's alive!' Sarah spun around and Nessie's eyes had opened!

In a great heave of motion, it raised itself up slowly from the beach and stared at the people who stood before it. It opened its gigantic mouth and roared. The roar echoed over the rocks and the sky and Max, Sarah and Megan covered their ears and stared at it in wonder. The creature raised its body more and more off the ground and let out a second bellowing cry.

'Look! There are more Nessies! Hundreds more!' cried Megan, clutching her father.

Sure enough, streaming through the icy water of the loch, towards the shore, were countless numbers of black, eel-like forms! It looked as though the whole lake had come alive with hundreds of slithering serpents! Megan watched, as numerous, humongous waves crashed towards the shore and towards Nessie. The waves swept over Nessie like the wind in a meadow and moments later, the water had pulled her back towards the loch. Every time one serpent advanced towards Megan, Sarah or Uncle Max, Nessie let out a bellow of warning. She was guarding them! For a few brief moments the shoreline seemed to be a writhing tangle of serpents. Then, as quickly as they had come, they were gone. Nessie too had plunged back into the lake, but not before giving its rescuers a brief thank you stare, to Max, Megan and Sarah.

Sarah smiled and slowly turned away and followed her bewildered cousin home. There was nothing but the dark, silent water left and its surface covered the deep secret below . . .

Leanne Moss (13)
Park High School, Colne

Sweet

There's a saying, that friends are your chosen family and at the tender age of 16, you begin to realise just how precious friends really are.

So, it's another Friday night, the pizza's ordered; the phone's off the hook and the video is set to play the soppiest movie in the house.

My friends are round and it's time to catch up on this week's latest gossip. Whilst the topic of boys is well underway, I realise how empty my life would be without each and every one of them. My friends have always been there for me, through the break-ups, make-ups and when the need to spend is becoming too big to handle alone.

Sam attacks me with the forbidden hair curlers. Ah, Sam, the lively one. I can remember the first day of secondary school, when nerves were at an all-time high. I was the only person I knew and I think it showed. Then along came a bouncy blonde, smiling and laughing, she simply took my hand and introduced me to the other girls.

That was five years ago, yet here we all are, just as close and just as strong.

The tissues have been dealt out, as Sam Wheat (aka Patrick Swayze) has just been shot in the all-time chick flick 'Ghost'.

Terri is the first to crack; she can be so caught up in a film, that it all becomes reality to her. I wonder what type of film her life story would make? Who would play the leading role? Could anyone, ever actually play her exactly as she is? Personally, I don't think anyone could, not even Hollywood's best actress! Terri is just, well, she's just Terri, the agony aunt, the sensitive soul and everyone's best friend. She couldn't be replaced. She is the first one I turn to in a crisis, for a reassuring cuddle and a 'let it all out' cry.

It's odd how we all just fuse together. I mean, we all have different personalities to the extreme, yet there have been no fights, no arguments and most important of all, no exclusions from the group. Is that what makes out friendship so strong? Is that why we have lasted for so long?

Something's wrong, I can sense it. We are all crying, but something tells me that Amy's tears are not from the sad news that lovely Patrick is now a ghost. No, her mind isn't on the film. She looks pale and is sat so stiffly on the most relaxing chair in the house.

Something is bothering her and I can see she is struggling to cope with it on her own. Nobody has noticed and at first I think I've made it all up in my head. I leave it for a while, but the thoughts just keep running through my head. I can't concentrate. I need an excuse for us to leave the room. I need an excuse. I can't believe I have to lie to my best friends, but I know this is something that doesn't need any more attention. Not yet at least.

'I'm going to make some drinks. Any requests?'

'Coke.'

'Yeah, same.'

'*Ssshhhh!*'

'Amy, can you help me?'

She gladly leaves her chair and steps into the kitchen. I turn round and give the biggest hug the world has ever known. The tears keep coming, streams and streams of them. My T-shirt is starting to feel warm and damp. I don't care and I can feel my eyes prickling and pretty soon I am in full flow too.

For about five minutes that is all we did. Where are the tissues when you really did need them?

Time for role reversal. How did Terri deal with my problems? I knew the perfect remedy.

The kettle is switched on; tea bags at the ready and the decent chocolate biscuits come out of the fridge. I pull out two chairs and we sit down for that good old chat that always seems to smooth out even the deepest creases.

I didn't need to say a word, our eyes communicate in a way I have never experienced before. This is serious. I knew it was serious.

'Amy?'

'Yeah, I know. I have to tell you something and I have spent weeks trying to figure out how to say it. I even practised in front of the mirror. How sad is that?'

A nervous laugh passes through us both.

'What is it? What's happened? Are you in trouble?'

'You could say that. I've got to go away. Something has happened and I can't stay . . .'

Claire Abbott (16)
Pendleton College, Salford

Gone

She was gone. Everything I had to live for was gone. My life now lived two thousand miles away from me. I was just a body, a lifeless body, roaming around this silent house. My soul was with her. My love was with her. I was nothing. She didn't seem to care about what she'd be leaving behind, the memories, the happy times we'd shared. She just couldn't wait to leave.

'I have to go,' she said, reaching down for her final bag.

My heart sank, like the remains of a beautiful ship wrecked at sea.

'I have to do this. It's best for both of us. We both need a fresh start,' she said, in a positive, yet uninterested tone.

Maybe she was right. Who would want to stay here, with a fat, middle-aged man like me? No aspirations, an unexhilarating job? A man that doesn't care if his clothes aren't ironed or if his socks aren't washed?

I managed to reluctantly force out the words, 'Take care then love,' as she grabbed the handle of the front door and swung it open, almost as if freedom awaited her.

'You too,' she shouted, as she strutted down the garden path, on the dull November day, as if sunlight was waiting at the broken gate, as if God had set the scene.

I watched her slender body walk away, until I could see it no more. The last vision I had of her felt like my last breath. That was it. My future had been taken away from me. I was the prisoner. She walked free.

I sat for what seemed like a lifetime in the armchair in our lounge. My lounge. My memories ran away with me. Memories that no matter how far away she was, *I* still had. Memories that no matter whether or not she forgot them, *I* would never. I *could* never.

It's been five years since her departure and I've had the occasional phone call from her and without fail, she would end by saying, 'I'm still here for you if you ever need me, you know that don't you?'

How can she be there for me if she's so far away? Living with some bloke she used to tell me was a 'friend from work'? Anyway, I'm coping. Yeah, I'm coping. I've quit my job and I still don't know how to work the washing machine, but well, I'm coping.

Most mornings I wake to find Tommy watching over me. Checking I'm alright. Day by day. He's been a good pal to me over the years. He's always there to listen to me or, at least, he acts as though he listens.

Every night before bed, I still climb into the attic and search for every last photo I have of her. Every last memory that I own. Every last moment of our lives together that we shared. Some nights I sit for hours looking at one photo. It doesn't matter which one, just as long as it has her face on it. Her bright, loving eyes, always in possession of a sparkle, that certain twinkle that separated her from many. Her flawless skin, always glowing as if sun-kissed all year round. Her smile, enough to light up anyone's darkest hour and bring a roar of happiness into anyone's life. If only it was mine once again. If only.

I'm coping though.

Winter drew nearer and the dark nights fell early. Things got worse. I felt as though if something didn't change in my life soon, if something good didn't happen to me in the next couple of days, well . . .

It was approaching seven o'clock on December 24th. I was sat in my usual evening position, in the armchair of the living room watching the Christmas television. I could not but resist putting up the Christmas decorations around the house. She loved them so much. Having the tinsel and fairy lights surrounding me gave me a sense of her presence.

Although I longed for her to be with me that evening, I was focusing my thoughts on how happy our Christmas' used to be in our house - how I would always burn the roast potatoes for Christmas dinner and how we would always make remarks about how dismal the jokes were in the crackers!

I got up to make myself a cup of cocoa before going to bed for an early night. I didn't want to stay awake upsetting myself about how good times used to be.

As I stirred my drink, watching the swirling image of the cocoa whizz around the cup, I heard a strange noise come from the front of the house. Tommy had raced to the door with a clear rush of acceleration running through him. I'd not seen his tail wag in excitement like it did that day for a very long time. As I approached the hall, I heard the front door swing open, just like all those years ago when she left.

'Merry Christmas, Dad. I'm back!'

Sarah Dickerson (16)
Pendleton College, Salford

The Meeting

The door slammed open. All activity stopped as the woman stepped inside, out from the cold, her long coat billowing behind her. Every eye fixed upon her shocking beauty; porcelain skin, smooth as silk, lips stained crimson, like blood, obsidian locks flowing in the motion of her stride, softy scented with the evening snow. Her cruel eyes met every stare whilst seeming distant and morose. The sadness echoed in her footsteps reverberating against the walls of the tavern. Not a sound disrupted the quiet beat her footfalls made against the wood, each note clear, crisp, yet fringed with mourning. Her glacier iris surveyed the anticipating crowd before flashing pearl-white fangs, discouraging any interference. With a feline grace, the beauty lifted her curved body up onto a towering stool close to the bar. Slowly, unsteadily at first, conversation began to return to the room. The intrusion made by the ghost-like woman, already fading from memory.

'Nothing changes,' she sighed under her breath, 'all these humans are the same; all this time their minds cannot comprehend my being.'

The beautiful creature sitting at the bar ordered a Bailey's and settled down to watch the cattle socialise, in the effort of gaining a modicum of pleasure. *Sickening,* thought the waiting huntress, *stomach churning!*

Again the door opened, letting a gust of freezing wind in to ruffle the midnight-black hair of the dark creature. The figure standing in the doorway was obscured; black clothing against the deepest blackness of night. Stepping aside, he closed the oaken door, sending out another wooden echo shattering many of the conversations held by the patrons of the bar. No emotion crossed the pale face of the newcomer, no sign of apology, or even the slightest hint of embarrassment. This man also looked around the softly lit room. His sapphire eyes glinting from the hollows of restless sockets, obscured by glasses that gave his face an air of intelligence.

The figure caught the gaze of the seated huntress and their eyes locked in place, as if by some ancient form of magic. Each of them stared into the other's soul and saw the darkness that lay, barely concealed, below a calm exterior. Each of them saw a part of themselves reflected there and knew peace . . . if only for a moment. A soft tinkling of glass broke the spell, slowly the standing figure moved across the room. His Dr Marten's British-made boots clashing against the hardwood floor, as his black long coat swirled the dust that carpeted the boards and made the motes dance in the candlelight.

Without asking, the newcomer placed himself unceremoniously upon the stool next to the woman. He ordered a Guinness from the pimply barboy who, while trying to create a shamrock, had spilled the black, creamy liquid down his trousers and was fumbling with a towel. The boy scurried away to avoid further mutterings of contempt given by the newcomer.

'Bloody incompetence,' he muttered, smiling before taking a long drink from the glass. He wiped the beer's foam from around his mouth with a satisfied smile. The two figures sat in silence, both nursing their respective drinks, neither one seeking to break the silence between them.

Finally, the woman spoke: 'You're different from these other cretins in here.'

'I'm glad you noticed,' replied the man, finishing off his drink and ordering another one.

The creature was angry at the man's matter-of-fact reply, but before she could reply, the man spoke again.

'I can say the same about you, Huntress,' he said, surprising her.

'You know what I am?' she asked, wearily.

'All I have to do is look,' continued the man, 'your demeanour suggests it. Every movement, every expression, the way in which you sip your drink and relish the taste, yet detest it.'

The huntress' curiosity was raised now and she continued, asking, 'Then why do you not run in fear, like one of these sheep would?'

'Simple. Because I am captivated by your beauty,' replied the man smoothly.

Despite the obvious tastelessness of the line, the huntress was taken aback. Her calm exterior suddenly breaking into a surprised expression that betrayed her entirely and the man let out a barely recognisable smile of triumph.

'What is your name, man?' she asked in a low voice.

The man turned, his eyes shining, a cruel smile passing over his lips and he moved closer. 'I am the one they call Lestatt,' replied the man, a smirk present on his lips, 'or do they call me Dracula?'

'The name is familiar, but not the face,' countered the huntress, sensing the joke, but not finding any humour in it, she smiled openly, *this creature, whatever he is, is infatuated,* she thought. *He will be worthy prey,* she mused, a plan formulating itself in her sharp mind. At last, she said, 'That was a tasteless joke my friend, I think you mock me.'

'No lady, you mock me by considering me as prey!'

The huntress was shocked. No mortal creature could see into her dead eyes and see her mind working. The plan she had hatched had been a masterpiece born of practise. For the first time in her long lifetime, the huntress knew fear.

Suddenly, the man stood. His great coat swirled around his ankles and sent more motes of dust cascading into the air. With no backward glance, his made his way towards the door. None of the tavern patrons looked in his direction. The door closed so quickly, that the only evidence of it having been open, was a rapidly melting snowflake, lying against the pine floorboards. The departure of the enigma left a bitter taste in the mouth of the huntress, that overpowered the sickly-sweet taste of the drink she had been consuming. Her dark eyes frowned into an even darker storm of contemplation. *Who was he? What was he?*

Questions floated in her mind's eye, twisting and revolving within her brain, but always the answers eluded her. Emotions, long forgotten and thought lost, welled up within her; anger, sorrow, pain, desire and confusion, all found a place within her, making her head spin with the strength of it all. The sensation was strong enough to almost surpass the exquisite joy of the hunt, as the crimson liquid drained from the prey and their frail bodies twisted and struggled, becoming weaker and weaker as the huntress' arousal grew.

Reality snapped back into place and with a flourish of her long coat, she raced out into the night after the strange man, praying that she wasn't too late.

Joseph Fairhurst (17)
Pendleton College, Salford

A Day In The Life Of . . .

I was swaying in the cool breeze with my brothers and sisters, the sun was shining, until a little girl came along and bent down, then she picked me out of the ground. I screamed and screamed. I screamed so hard, one of my petals nearly fell off. The pain was excruciating and I didn't even say goodbye to my family.

The pain soon wore off and I realised I was flying around the forest. Something was wrapped around my delicate skin. I stopped at a really big thing and we went inside. It said something to a creature, but I don't know what. It filled something with water and put me in it. They put me on a flat surface.

The water was cool and refreshing, but I wanted to go home. I watched them eat and walk past me, with a cool breeze. I cried every night just wishing to go back and feel the soil in my roots.

Soon she came back with some of my family. I was happy to see them. They were put in the same water and we talked and talked. They were saying how painful it was. I was happy now, my yellow petals so bright. I was never sad anymore. Sometimes I cried, as I really missed my mum.

Sarah Trueman (11)
Pensby High School for Girls, Wirral

A Day In The Life Of . . .

My life begins as a blinding, flashing light. I am the last of my kind, so I'm taken to the dark room. Next thing I know, I am being saturated, then hung to drip bone dry. Now I'm packaged with my fellows. I await for my creator to collect me.

The doorbell jingles and my owner is here to pick me up. I am taken to a dark place, far away from here. Later on I hear people around me. Then I'm being looked at by several faces. I am put into a plastic case with others above and below me.

I was being passed around the room and people were saying things about me. People were laughing, pulling ugly faces as if they didn't like the way I look. I felt so small. They were saying that I'm funny, ugly and they were prodding their fingers on top of me. But people also complimented me too. Saying I'm pretty nice, could do better and that's good enough for me.

Sometimes I see my fellows up high, with golden outlines which surround them. I am looked at by eight or nine different faces each day. I always feel so popular! Everyone looking at me and nobody else looking at the others!

If you haven't figured it out yet, then 'surprise!' I'm a photograph! I have many smiles on my face too!

Charlotte Collins (11)
Pensby High School for Girls, Wirral

A Day In The Life Of . . .

I lie in a ripped cardboard box, never seeing the light of the outside world, until one day I'm horribly awoken by bumping down what I think is a ladder, followed by the bumpy stairs. My fellow friends are slowly following behind, in a squished cardboard box.

The first thing I see when I wake up, is the menacing face of a two-year-old boy, pulling and tugging at all my emerald-green branches. I am slowly pulled up by humongous, sweaty hands. Now, I am getting fitted together and all my branches are being pulled apart and spread out, so they are ready for humans to hang things on them.

Afterwards, my friend, the angel, is placed on the top of my head. My branches and head begin to ache under the weight of the many decorations being hung on me. I start to begin to feel hot and sweaty. My eyes sting as strange things keep flashing on and off.

I try to fall asleep, but I can never rest. Items start to go fuzzy and I feel like I am going to collapse. I suddenly fall to the hard ground, all I can hear is a child crying and an ear-aching noise. What seemed like many hours passed and I couldn't open my eyes. I feel myself being lifted back into place.

The humans overload me again with all decorations making my arms ache even more!

It's a hard life being a Christmas tree!

Olivia McKernan (11)
Pensby High School for Girls, Wirral

A Day In The Life Of . . .

The first thing I am aware of in the warm, cloud-free mornings, are the children walking and talking around me. I know their faces very well, as I see them for about two hours a day. Some of them are very pleasant, they are the youngest children though. They give me things that are very appetising. They just pop it into my mouth and I swallow it whole. But the older children are appalling. They just desert their delicious food on the cold floor. They don't care about me. They just can't be bothered and just dump the luscious food on the floor!

I look forward to days when they feed me healthy things. I especially like apple cores and orange peel and if I'm really lucky, I'll be in for a nice ripe banana, but oh dear, most of the children think I want crisp packets and sweet wrappers. These are no good for *my* delicate stomach.

At the end of the day, it all goes quiet. I feel neglected sometimes, just standing there alone, with nobody to talk to. I am alone now.

The caretaker has just come - he comes every day, after all the loud children have gone. He shoves the last pieces of rubbish into our mouths. Then he comes and takes a big, black bag which holds all my tasty food. Then I am hollow, empty, ready to start a new day.

Rebecca Edwards (12)
Pensby High School for Girls, Wirral

A Day In The Life Of . . .

I woke, along with my fellows, my top aching and instantly my innards take effect. So, *hic,* if you haven't guessed, my innards are alcohol and *hic,* I am the bottle. A gin bottle to be precise and I live in Raffles Hotel in Singapore, *hic.* The bar opens at 12 midday, so I sit waiting gleefully, *hic,* watching the glasses being washed, they hate that. Slowly, the clock's limbs trudge towards midday and the first customers roll in.

A young man, about 20, arrives and sits down, *hic*. His eyes roll over myself and the whiskey. I know his face I think. Then it comes to me, this man came here for a party, after a marriage. By the looks of things, he has had a break-up. In storms the bride and she looks so tired, I swear she would simply drop to the floor. Her face is growing more thunderous by the minute. A row breaks out over what seems to be money and a divorce, they race out, raging, fuming, if you will, *hic.* They enter once more and the woman grabs me by the neck and hurls me across the room at the man. He dodges this attack and I, *hic,* smash into a million pieces on the floor!

I wish I could tell you what happened to these two, but that is it, as I am no more.

Helen Sheridan (11)
Pensby High School for Girls, Wirral

A Day In The Life Of . . .

The primary thing I was aware of, was a wet sensation gliding down my smooth spine. It suddenly went, but was briskly substituted with a water-logged experience. It soon occurred to me that I was being dunked back and forth into a bowl of very strong-smelling liquid.

Soon it came to a halt and I felt myself being thrown aside onto a solid metal plate, alongside all of the machinery. It is a traumatising life for my family and I, as we are thrown everywhere and are shown no respect in the slightest.

It is a Wednesday today and is one of the busiest days ever. We have so many patients depending on us to do a good job. Today, Mrs Brown is paying her regular visit and by golly, does her breath smell! My colleagues and I usually faint at just the sight of her.

'Here I am, dear!' cried a voice that sounded strangely like Mrs Brown's. 'Should I sit on the chair?' Mrs Brown quizzed.

'Yes dear, do sit down. Make yourself comfortable,' answered the master. Then, the moment we had all been dreading . . . Mrs Brown unlocked her pursed lips and let out her dreaded fumes. Fumes poisonous enough to make one drop down dead!

I entered it with my colleague and together we went on a long and unforgettable journey into Mrs Brown's mouth. I needed air, my rear mirror was fogging up. I couldn't see daylight! Would I get out alive? On the other hand, would the awful gas kill me anyway? I did not know.

'Oh, that blasted mirror keeps fogging up, so I can't see any of your teeth at all Mrs Brown, do excuse me one second,' complained the dentist. With that, he wiped it with his uniform. 'Right, let's try again, shall we?'

Clare Elizabeth Algawi (12)
Pensby High School for Girls, Wirral

A Day In The Life Of . . .

There I was, brand new, blinking at the world around me. I could see my family all creamy and exquisite. A tall person peeked through the glass door and turned the key. Straight away I was lifted into the air and placed, looking out to the world.

Business had begun. A small girl, about five years old, pointed at me through the glass, eyes big and blue. Her mother shuffled behind and smiled. The door opened wide and a big gust of wind blew through. I was bundled in a box and handed over.

It was pitch-black. I was splodging everywhere, but then the worst came, I was put in a big, metal monster; a car. I was knocked everywhere, *bits* of me going everywhere. The box opened. Light flooded in and a big finger prodded me. I heard shouting and the chubby girl started to cry. Once again I was put in the dark and battered.

The journey was horrible. I was everywhere. The box was opened and I was carefully restored to my original state. I was carried through to a big room, that had a huge table in the middle. A huge china disk was under me and I was placed on it. An incredibly sharp instrument was stuck into me and I was put into a cold room for about two hours with other cold beings. Once I was taken out, I was placed on the huge table not knowing what to do.

So, here I am now, still not knowing what to do, waiting for something to happen . . .

Lisle Taylor (11)
Pensby High School for Girls, Wirral

A Day In The Life Of A Baked Bean

It was on Friday the 13th of May when it happened, I should have known I would have bad luck on that day!

I was stuck in the tin, squashed with all my friends, when the lid opened and we got poured into a bowl. We got put into a large box and the door of the box was closed. It got very warm. This loud *ping* sounded and the door opened. We were so glad to get out of that horrible box.

Then we got surrounded by big humans, around a table. They all picked up their spoons and put the spoon into the dish where me and my mum were holding hands, scared. As the spoon got my mum, I screamed. I shouted and shouted for my mum to come back.

She had gone. There was no way to bring her back. The spoon grabbed me, but I didn't try to escape, I was too upset. I got swallowed and there was my mum, in this human's stomach. I ran up to her and gave her a big hug.

That's what happened up until now, this is where I'm writing from, the human's stomach!

Lisa Cunniffe (12)
Pensby High School for Girls, Wirral

A Day In The Life Of . . .

Well, here I am, stuck on a tree, waiting to be picked. I am in luck! Here is the farmer to pick my friends and me ready to be harvested.

After I was picked, I was washed in lovely cold water (it is nice after you have been lying in the hot, burning sun). So then I taste nice and then I look nice. Then a pair of wet hands grabbed me and put me into a big, dark, gloomy box, with my friends and family.

Suddenly, I could feel a rumble. I guessed that we were moving, moving in a huge van, which passes my home every day! This was a once in a lifetime experience (but little did I know it was!) It was a very, very bumpy ride. My sister even turned purple at the beginning of the ride. But in the second half, she turned green again, otherwise they would have thrown her away! Finally, we arrived at a peculiar place. It had thousands of people, with baskets and trolleys and then my mum told me that we were in the place called the supermarket. Then we were put in some boxes with no lids, it was bright, but the only thing wrong was that I was separated from my family. But I was still with my friends!

Different people picked me up, it tickled! Then this little baby girl said to her mum, 'Can I have this one?'

Her mum replied, 'Yes, if you want that one.'

So I was in these hot hands and got thrown into a basket, as the girl dropped me out of her hand. In this rusty old basket, I noticed my family passing by, they were very pleased to see me.

Once we had been bought, I was put in a car. This was very uncomfortable again, because I kept sliding from left to right and back and forth!

Afterwards, I was placed in a bowl with other strange-looking things, some of them were orange and others were long and yellow. I waited and waited for someone to rescue me. Soon after I was saved. Someone came and picked me up and put me in this slobbery, slimy hole. Big claws gripped me, as the hole started to get bigger I got smaller, until I started to get eaten! So here I am, in a person's stomach and this is my life story.

And by the way, I am an apple!

Kimberley Smith (11)
Pensby High School for Girls, Wirral

A Day In The Life Of . . .

When I was young, my mother always used to remind me, in a forceful voice, to 'Never, ever step over the line'. I never used to understand what it meant, until *it* happened, then it became crystal clear.

My friends and myself were playing a traditional children's game, hide-and-seek. It used to annoy all the elders, they used to complain, but we did it anyway! Then it happened, I dashed around the corner, once I had run to hide, but tripped and fell. I landed on an ankle I had previously hurt. It was throbbing and throbbing. Then I remembered about the line and that I was moving rapidly away from my home, friends, childhood, but most importantly, my family. They were fading in the distance, never to be seen again.

I panicked and panicked, but that didn't get me anywhere! I had guessed that my family probably didn't even know I had left. Long stalks shaded me and different colours surrounded me in this unfamiliar place. The stalks swayed in the breeze. I collapsed down and sobbed and in no time my feet were drenched in a stream of sorrow! One creature noticed me, he seemed to be the only one around. Slowly he approached me, 'It's alright, it's alright.' He said his name was Englebert. He used to be a chief once and had owned his own tribe until a huge argument and a colossal war had broken out. Apparently, they'd all stepped over the line, just as I had done. Englebert and I had a great time. I had totally forgotten about where I was and where my family were. We played tig and we also feasted on our surroundings. It was the best dinner I had had in a long time!

Englebert was a kind soul, who would always put others first. Hours passed by and Englebert and I became better and better friends by the minute.

The afternoon had forced its way on. We were on the move again, until a white, foamy substance stopped us in our tracks. Gradually, it started to eat away at our legs and arms. I screamed and shouted, 'Help, what's going on?' A tremendous flood of water came rushing in. I was terrified. I was swept into a dirty, rotten, smelly drain, where I was never to be seen again.

Who said it was an easy life being a nit?

Alexandra Power (12)
Pensby High School for Girls, Wirral

A Day In The Life Of . . .

First thing, when I wake up in the morning on a cold, hard floor, with a thin sheet over me, I think, well, I don't even have to think to myself, because I have been like this since I was 11 years old. But I cannot resist the taste, it is so succulent, your life passes before your eyes, but anyway, I still think this thought to myself. Once again I am going to be sitting by myself, all alone, no one to talk to, no friends, nothing. No one will help me for free, it all costs. Why is life like this? I may as well kill myself. No I cannot do this. Just one more sip, it won't hurt me, help me, help me, what shall I do? It cannot be someone approaching me, who can it be? Someone to help me, someone to be my friend, *wow* it cannot be! They grabbed me with their sweaty palms, they would not let me go, I shouted, 'No, get off me.'

They said to me in a kind, sweet voice, 'It's OK, we have come to help you.'

'Give me them back, they're mine, not yours!'

I got taken away in this white and blue van or something. It was warm in the thing and nice and cosy. The van jolted to a halt and then they took me out and said, 'It's OK, calm down, you will be safe here.'

They put me down in this warm chair. There were lots of people talking to me, being friends with me. The people that had brought me here, had gone. They helped me through. Now I am normal and have lots and lots of friends.

I was a drug addict.

Tasha Stubbs (11)
Pensby High School for Girls, Wirral

A Day In The Life Of . . .

I woke up with nothing but coldness under my thin jacket, with only a thin sheet to cover me, knowing it wouldn't be enough to keep me warm.

It was cold and windy, paper blowing, bins rolling around, banging against the graffiti-covered walls. I looked at the town's clock, it read 6.35am. A bin lorry drove past, making an even bigger draught, making me shiver even more.

I sat up with a long needle in my hand and a tourniquet tied tightly around my arm. About to inject, I had the needle a centimetre away from my arm, I stopped to think to myself, *why had it come to this?* I knew it was because of my mother. She killed herself because she suffered from depression. She was on medication for years, but it got too much for her after my brother started smoking when he was 11, to top it all off, my dad ran off with some barmaid from the pub next door, so I left and here I am on the streets.

I started again, steadied my arm, had the vein in view and pushed the needle into my arm. I immediately started to feel drowsy and lay on the ground motionless.

I slowly opened my eyes, seeing double. I felt better, stronger and more alive than usual. I steadily stood up, holding on to a pipe sticking out of the wall for extra support, I walked off. A woman and a kid walked past, she gave me a funny look and walked off without a care in the world. I wanted to chase after her and give her a piece of my mind, only it was a bit hard to see where I was going and I walked into a lamp post. I shouted, 'You shouldn't be there,' and walked off. Then alarmed and silent, I stood rooted to the spot, trying to make out the double figure, stood two shops away. It was my dad, I'm sure it was. I heard his deep voice, 'Thanks love.' After 12 years he'd decided to come back. Now, of all times, when my depressed mother's dead.

I went over about to say something, but the words wouldn't come out. I stood there, with my mouth open. He looked down at me with disgust, not knowing who I was. That look made me so angry. He walked off down the road.

'I am your son.'

He looked round, wondering who that drugged-up psycho was speaking to. He finally realised I was speaking to him. He ran over and said to me, 'Have you completely lost your mind? My son was a kind boy who concentrated on his school work.'

I didn't know what to do, it just came out, it never meant to. 'Yeah, maybe when I was six, until you ran off with that barmaid from the pub next door. You left all three of us behind. Do you know Mum died five years ago, because of your other son, James. He wasn't such an angel either, was he?'

I walked off and tried to forget that the conversation had taken place. I was in pieces. I decided to go back to my alley and go to sleep. I read the town's clock again, it read 9.59pm. I snuggled up as much as I could and fell asleep.

Next morning at 9.12am, I wrapped the tourniquet round my arm so the vein was in view and pushed the long, thin needle into the vein. Going through the same routine, I felt drowsy and started to see double.

Here is some advice: *never start on drugs,* no matter how cool you think it is. I am a stupid idiot, who lost his way to live and here I am, on the streets with nothing but a worn out quilt and one set of clothes and of course, my daily injection kit. *Don't you be like me!* Now you know how it is to spend *a day in the life of . . . a drug addict.*

Amy Dallinger (12)
Pensby High School for Girls, Wirral

A Day In The Life Of . . .

As I awake in the morning, I have my family all around me. All my brothers and sisters are fighting about who's going this morning. We all like playing with the prize, which is inside with us! I like the colour of me because I look very tanned. I am a sort of chocolate-brown colour. Do you know what I am yet?

Well, I live in a kind of dark place, it is always dark until about a minute of when we see light and some of my family just disappear where the light is. Whenever that happens, the light shines down on us, we just sit there praying. There is only one day a year that the light doesn't shine down on us, but we don't know when that is!

My mum is not alive anymore, because she got crushed and died. That was a long time ago. I look after the rest of the family with my dad.

None of my family go to work, that is why we are quite poor. That is bad because we have the biggest family in the world, I don't have to go to school, I don't really know what it is, but my dad said it is just a waste of time and you don't learn anything from just sitting down all day in school. I think the reason he was telling me this was because even if I did want to go, I couldn't. I am a Coco Pop!

Pippa Laurie (12)
Pensby High School for Girls, Wirral

A Day In The Life Of . . .

One day, I woke up in this giant bed with others around me, they looked exactly like me. When I looked up, I saw a big one that provided me with my milk, so I could stay alive.

A few weeks later, I was able to walk and I was walking everywhere, but one day a large hand picked me up and I got carried over to another hand and was being passed around a lot. Then I got wrapped up in a warm blanket and carried outside, I then went on a rocky, bumpy car journey and I felt a bit sick, but managed to fall asleep! When we got out of the car, I was put on the floor and left to sleep in a bed just like the one I had left behind, where my brothers and sisters and also my mother was.

A month passed and I was old enough to go for walks outside, so my owner put my lead on and took me out for a walk to the park. Whilst we were in the park, I was let off my lead and allowed to run around, (as long as I came back when my owner shouted me!) When I got called it was playtime over outside, so my owner put my lead back on and we went home. I did that trip nearly every day and I was taken to the vet to be checked on every so often!

A few years passed and I was getting old and tired and I couldn't really be bothered to do much, but I still had to keep fit, so I just went up the road and back again.

Then one day I was left to do what I wanted, so I just stayed in my bed all day. I did live a very happy life, but now it was time to let that all go!

Stephanie O'Connell (12)
Pensby High School for Girls, Wirral

A Day In The Life Of . . .

I wait in the darkness; it is six o'clock in the morning. There is no sound or movement. My fellow friends glisten, as the moonlight catches on the window. I stand on my evergreen floor without moving an inch and wait until the clock chimes seven.

Finally, three pairs of feet tiptoe down the stairs. I cannot wait to see their glowing faces, when they see the treasures that I behold. Slowly the door opens, my family run inside, their smiles growing by the minute. Their glee is expressed by the frantic ripping of paper. The packaging is removed and the booty is handled with care.

As the parents come down, they have black shadows under their eyes as they have not slept a wink. The family are still in their snug pyjamas, but they show love and care. I would wish to have a family like this! I stay firm at my base, they never notice me blink, or even move.

Throughout the cold winter's day, old and young, short and tall, people pass by the window, admiring my beauty then walking on, snuggling in their heavy coats. But, they all take a glimpse at me in my majestic crimson gown.

Hang on a minute, what is happening? Someone grabs me and places me into an old, ripped, cardboard box. Next go my friends, all one by one. I will have to wait another year before I am the fairy on the top of the Christmas tree again!

Abigayil Thomas (12)
Pensby High School for Girls, Wirral

A Day In The Life Of . . .

Today I was very rudely woken up by my mother, but I snuggled up to her and begged for food until Mum poured out my fave crunchies. I gulped half down and went outside for a walk. When I came back I found Riley licking my bowl clean, luckily I had caught a snack outside. I put it down and decided to show off to everyone, but when I turned around, my mum carried it off in a dustpan saying, 'Hermione, that was mean!'

After the others left, leaving Riley inside, I went off for a walk. As I passed my neighbours, they started clucking, 'Mice, mice.'

So I pounced into their garden and started looking around.

'Ha, ha, we only have eggs,' quacked Mortimer.

I stormed off and ran down to Harvey my friend and he had fish in one of his many houses. We then snuck up to the beehives and licked up some of the honey.

As me and Harvey headed to the ditch, Tom, the street boss, stood in front of us and he had Sophie with him (one of his gang). We had a major fight, it ended up with me and Harvey running away.

After a long day hunting, we each went home to tea. When I got back, Mum shut the door and gave me and Riley dinner, then Alice picked me up and put me in the carrier. She took me to the car and Riley followed, this meant one thing, the vet!

As we got there, Riley whined. We waited in a room, then we started to move towards the room. They put me on the table and gave me and Riley an injection. Riley tried to get out the door and I tried to get in the carrier, but the pain of the pointed needle hurt us.

When we got home, I ate all my food and snuggled onto Mum's bed, until she picked me up, put me in my room and shut the door and flicked the lights off. I then curled up into my bed, which is blue with a paw print pattern and is shaped like an igloo.

Alice Tordoff (11)
Pensby High School for Girls, Wirral

A Day In The Life Of . . .

I have been many places and eaten many things. I have been east, west, north and south. Let me tell you about the time I was in England.

I was on the floor eating when a monster pounced on me and caught me in its claws. I tried to get away, but it hung on with its sharp teeth and slit eyes.

Suddenly, the black four-legged monster ran away. I thought, *this is strange, it has never done that before,* (the monster had cut me). There was a tall block with windows and doors.

A thing came out one of those door, all my friends called it a human. It came up to me and said, 'Aren't you a lovely creature? You have lovely eyes. Oh, you poor thing. That cat gave you a broken wing. Don't worry, I will take care of you.'

It put me in a box with food and water for six days and six nights. I got attached to the human. It had long hair and a pale face with blue clothing.

The next day, she opened the box and took me outside. I looked into her blue, glowing eyes. She said, 'Go, you are free, your wing has healed. Go on little robin, leave.'

I flew away, but I came straight back. I could not leave her. So now her and I are great friends. We stay and play in the garden. The memories last for a lifetime of fun.

So, now you know my story and I have been here for many years and she is the one who gave me my name, Frizzy.

Alisha Davies (11)
Pensby High School for Girls, Wirral

A Day In The Life Of . . .

Crawling along the cold, damp wooden floor, towards a wooden box with the word 'candy' carved on it. As I look at the box I feel hungry and my mouth waters, because of the thought of candy. I climbed up the box and fell on top of delicious gobstoppers. As I started to feast on this delicious snack, a human hand picked me up. I tried to escape, but it was too late, the gobstopper and I fell into a wet, red place! I looked around, when all of a sudden, a gust of wind blew me.

The gobstopper and I came tumbling out of the human mouth. I fell on top of a huge colony of me. We all headed for home, with the gobstoppers and some sugar. We all had a lovely meal, with a very nice desert called lollipops. I do not know why they are called lollipops, but all I know is that they are absolutely gorgeous.

Next thing I know, a huge spray of liquid came out of nowhere. Everyone was dying. I tried my best to save them, but I was nearly dying as well. I ran back to our home and hid. One hour later, I saw dead bodies all over the place. There I was, on my own, looking at everyone dying everywhere. Can you guess who I am? I am an ant.

Sophie Kirkham (11)
Pensby High School for Girls, Wirral

A Day In The Life Of . . .

I woke up this morning and I felt very sore. I got a big lashing from yesterday. I didn't feel like entertaining people, doing tricks for them. Those cruel people watching me suffer, just for fun. They don't realise that my keepers whip me if I don't feel very well, some animals can die because of the poor state that they live in. I have managed to survive for a few years, but I haven't been here for very long. I am meant to lie in the sun and enjoy myself with the other animals, like me, but no, no, no, I am a circus tiger. Nothing can help me out of here.

I do enjoy acting for the little children and seeing their little faces in amazement.

A nice, kind man was interested in buying me for £3,000, but the keeper of the circus said that he would think about the offer, but he wouldn't promise anything and to come back the next day.

It was the big day and I had butterflies in my tummy. I might be going to live in a safari park from now on. The keeper actually said yes. Yes, yes, yes, yes!

When I saw the safari park, it was my biggest dream, now I could have a big run around and make the kids happy. They loved me, I was their favourite tiger. From now on I will never get whipped ever, ever again.

Robyn Hall (12)
Pensby High School for Girls, Wirral

A Day In The Life Of . . .

I am at the top of my tree, eating some of our apples, near my other friends. I like my feathers, they are beautiful. They have different colours.

The breeze is calm at the top of the tree, but it's roasting hot in the sunshine. Hmmm, I can smell ripe plums on the plum tree.

It's great flying. I can fly so high I can, without anyone stopping me.

Ssshh, what's that noise in the gum tree? Is it danger? Good job that I have got green on me, nothing will see me.

Oh, it's only a koala in the gum tree. I won't even dare go in that gum tree. Koalas are lonely and cranky. I hate when animals scare me with their noises.

I will fly away and go to another tree. It's great being a parrot. There are different kinds of parrots in Australia. I am a Rosella parrot. I am red, green, yellow and blue.

I am beautiful when you see me or hear me, I will probably speak to you. It's wonderful when I see different animals, but they are scary.

When going to sleep, it's very hard because other parrots sing or fight, even the other animals are doing the same things.

When waking up it's really the same thing every day. Looking for food, standing next to my family and friends. It's great and fantastic, but also boring being a parrot.

Paul Norton (15)
Roundwood High School (MLD), Manchester

A Day In The Life Of . . .

Here I am back on the snow. I have to pull sledges for people with my friends, but I have strong legs, so I can pull. I live in Antarctica with my friends and my family. It is cold in Antarctica, but I have thick fur so I don't get cold. I am like a dog, but I can't bark.

When I am pulling the sledge, the people whip me so I can go faster for them. I wish I could live in another country, where there's warmth and I don't get whipped all the time when I am pulling the sledge.

When I am hungry, I walk about looking for food which the people have leftover or for fish in the water.

When there's a load of luggage on the sledge, the man harnesses me to the sledge with the other eight. The man stops us when we need a rest.

We don't live in kennels. Our masters live in igloos or houses but we have to sleep outside. When it is time for us to go to bed, all my friends and family cuddle up together so we can keep warm

Tomorrow morning I have to pull the sledge on my own for the master, so I have to go to bed early tonight.

Ryan Purdy (14)
Roundwood High School (MLD), Manchester

A Day In The Life Of A Goldfish

In June 2002, there was a fair on at Withenton Park. I saw people walking by, looking at all of us.

A little boy won the choice of a goldfish or a teddy and he chose me! I swam about in excitement, because I was going to a new home.

I was taken to a glass tank. Through my bag I saw lots of goldfish like myself. I was let into the huge tank and I swam towards the other goldfish. We got on straight away. I thought that I was in paradise.

We get fed twice a day! I can hide if I need some peace. We all come in different sizes, but I am the biggest of the bunch. We shine when we go past the light. We blow bubbles in the water and move our fins and tails. We can change colour. I can turn black, white, gold and yellow. I love where I live, where I live under the water, but I hate being caught in a net and put in a plastic bowl, then back in the tank. This happens unexpectedly about once a month.

Thomas Bradley (15)
Roundwood High School (MLD), Manchester

A Day In The Life Of . . .

My master is loading me up. I can get very moody. I spit in his face. I travel for days without drinking. Sometimes, we race in the desert. I am brown and furry. I carry bags on my back. I can run fast, but it is hot in the desert. I hate it when we have strong winds, the sand blows in my face and stings my eyes.

There are strange shapes up ahead. I think they are called rocks. There is no rainfall, I wish it would, because it is so hot. I hate it when my master hits me with a stick.

Sometimes, we have to go for a long walk in a caravan. We are in a line. I make a noise, because there is a camel up ahead, I hate the other camels. We fight and spit at each other.

We are walking and need a drink. We are having so much luck, over there I can see an oasis of trees. Yes, water!

Pamela Wood (15)
Roundwood High School (MLD), Manchester

A Day In The Life Of A Rat

Oh no, look at the time. Better hurry up before I get killed by the *big* cars. My stomach is rumbling. I need food. *Mmm* same old burger. This is a bit of my breakfast.

Oh no, *alien.* Quick, into here, a safe place. Some more of that beautiful food. Burgers, what are these long things? Are they an animal just like me? Oh no, I think I need a bit of help here. It's getting to my nice home. I think that it is this way. Hold on, it is this way. Is it this way?

These people don't seem to see me, because I'm very small. All the way down this long road.

Time is ticking away, getting hungry, sleepy. Need to find my home. Oh no, rain, need shelter fast. *Cats!* I can see cats everywhere, hissing. They are going to eat me! Oh gosh, it doesn't matter now. *Phew!* Yeah, that's right, go inside now. Oh no, still raining! What? Where has that nasty rain gone? Good, go home you nasty thing!

Is that a bin over there? *Yes, yes!* More food. Don't like this other animal taste! *Yuck!* Spit it out *quick!* But I like this square shape with the orangey colour. That was nice. I feel nearly full up now. The only thing is . . . finding my true home.

Graham Neild (15)
Roundwood High School (MLD), Manchester

A Day In The Life Of . . .

I wake up, crawl out of my hole and follow my friends into the tunnels. I hate it when people put some powder over my hole. It burns like acid. Most of my family have died or got injured. But I love going on long walks in the grass, it's great because people can't see me and children can't pick me up and squash me in their hands. Anyway, back to my story. I love the exquisite smell of flowers and I love to explore other parts of my country. I love playing hide-and-seek with my pals! I'm really good at hiding in the grass. I love hiding in the gorgeous flowers and I love deep flowers, because it's much harder to find me. Also, I love the smell.

Suddenly, I'm whisked away. My world is shaking! I have to hold on for dear life. It is like an earthquake. The flower shakes again, then it stops. I'm thinking, *yes, I'm alive!* Then I see a massive shadow. I hear a sniffing noise. I am being sucked up! It stops and the flower turns upside down and I am hanging on to a petal. Oh no! I can't hold on any more. I'm fallingggggg . . .

I just drop through thin air, it is just like a roller coaster ride. My stomach feels like butterflies. I land safely on the ground and I see a spider! It starts chasing me. I run into a spider's trap. Oh no! I am stuck in his web. I say to the spider, 'Are you going to eat me?'

The spider looks at me. I see his long tongue and his eyes, glowing red. He is not blinking. He runs into me and he wraps me up in his sticky, soft thread. I think this is the end of me.

Luke Cameron (15)
Roundwood High School (MLD), Manchester

A Day In The Life Of . . .

I open my eyes in the morning breeze. I stride down to the watering hole, leading my thirsty pride. The other animals quickly run to the other side of the river, scared of being eaten. We spy a zebra! I crawl on the desert plain. My pride are hungry and we are keeping low, trying not to make a sound. I jump out and pounce on the zebra, dragging him down. He struggles and nearly escapes, but the other lions chase him and kill him. We bring the raw meat to the pride and we start to eat it.

Suddenly, a pack of greedy, savage hyenas try to get our zebra. They are laughing at us. I roar at the hyenas, growling and showing my teeth. One of the hyenas is growling at me and I jump forward and scratch the leader and they go back. We beat them again!

Then we all get up and move to a shady tree. I clean my cubs. We are alive for another day.

Natasha Gasper (14)
Roundwood High School (MLD), Manchester

A Day In The Life Of . . .

In the morning I wake up on an empty stomach. The sun is shining, hot as usual in the day. I go down to the waterhole for a drink. Then I go and search for something to eat. I like my food very chewy and tasty. I normally like zebras, but I want to find something easier, to catch my prey.

I hide in some tall bushes and sniff the air. When the prey gets close enough I launch myself at them, using my sharp claws to stab them into the flesh. When I stab them deep enough, the prey starts to slow down. When the prey is nearly dead, I start to chew on the warm flesh. When I am nearly full, I go and get another drink from the waterhole.

After I have had something to drink, I go and lie down under a tree. I take a nap, under the sun, shaded by the tree. While lying down, I can see in the distance, trees. I can even see herds of elephants passing by, but the easiest catch I can see is giraffes eating the leaves off the trees.

The sun's heat is creating a heat haze all around me. Far away from me, it is making me a bit dizzy and also sleepy and dozy. My other friends lie down with me and we rest. I normally play fight, but sometimes they take it too seriously and end up having a real fight. Every fight I have had I have won.

I like to be alone, but my friends like to help me out. I have got three little cubs and I always look after them, because my female lion was killed by an elephant. My favourite colours are orange, white and black.

David Spilsbury (15)
Roundwood High School (MLD), Manchester

A Day In The Life Of . . .

I slide along on my belly, out of the grass. I stick out my tongue to taste the air. There's something small to my left. I slither on the ground, towards the smell, sticking out my tongue now and again to taste the air. I'm near the smell. I have to be quiet if I want to eat.

I stick out my tongue. The air smells like a rat was here. I go in the direction where the smell is strongest. I stick out my tongue. I can nearly taste the rat.

I slide behind it, quietly. I coil up ready to strike. I lunge myself forwards, fangs sticking out, ready to send venom into the victim. The rat is dead!

I unhinge my lower jaw and use my fangs to eat the rat. I can move my fangs separately to eat the corpse. It takes a long time to digest the rat. I don't have to eat for another month.

I slide back towards my den in the grass. I make a spiral shape with my body and go to sleep, still digesting the rat.

Zak Shankland (15)
Roundwood High School (MLD), Manchester

A Day In The Life Of A Cat

Budge up, I need to sit down somewhere you know! Fine, if I can't sit on the chair, I'll sit on you instead! Oh, you've got really bumpy legs which, by the way, I can't be doing with. I'll just have to press the lumps out then . . . there we are! Nice and flat! Ahhh, peace at last! So warm . . . so cosy . . . so . . .

Argh! What a rude awakening! Don't you *dare* push me on the flo . . . ow! *Fine!* I'm going outside! Hsss! I don't need you and your bumpy legs! Ohh . . . it's chilly out here. Shall I go back inside? No, they've shut the door on me. Typical, just typical! Hey, hold the Felix! What's this? A stranded mole? Perfect! Come to Buttons, Mr Mole, I'm hungry!

I can't believe that pesky little runt escaped my claws! *Gasp!* What's this I hear? That wretched mole, plodding along the floor? I've got you now you little . . . big? Moles aren't big! Unless . . .

Oh no! It's the neighbour's evil Rottweiler, Scamp! Don't you look at me like that! I am *not* a toy! *Not* a toy! Hsss! Hsss! Okay, that did *not* work! Back up, Bad Breath! Leave me alone! Is that your owner calling? Leave me be you big . . . nice . . . dog! Look, I've told you to go away. *Now!* Okay, never mind, I think the best thing to do now is *run!*

Tree! Ha, ha, you can't climb trees, you idiotic, incompetent idiot!

Woah! That was hard! Only problem is, I'm afraid of heights! C'mon Buttons! Pull yourself together! What was that? Ha! That's my owner! That's right! Kick that Scruff - sorry, Scamp!

Ahhh . . . bliss. So warm . . . so cosy . . . so . . .

Bethany Byrom (12)
St Bede's RC High School, Blackburn

A Day In The Life Of A Professional Wrestler

It's almost my turn to step into the ring. This match means everything to me. It's been 9 years of blood, sweat and tears and finally I get my shot at the World Heavyweight Championship, but everything comes with a price. I must go one on one with a 7 foot, 500lb monster. He goes by the name of 'The Slayer'. He definitely lives up to his name. For many years I've watched him end careers in one simple match. This feud has been three years in the making.

Me and this man used to share a common bond. We used to be friends until 3 years ago. We were set to face each other and he kicked me so hard, he broke my legs in three places, putting me out of work for a year.

This guy knows he won't be able to put me away that easily, I know he is intimidated by me. I've been put through tables, pushed off ladders and busted open.

Tonight it will all be settled. Will I become the best in the business? Will I turn the tables and slay The Slayer?

Here I go, making my way to the ring. Wish me luck.

Matthew Tennant (13)
St Bede's RC High School, Blackburn

A Day In The Life Of A Drawing Pin

The sun beams down on the white, sandy beach as children play in the crystal water. There are cooler boxes full of sand-filled sandwiches, sunburnt smiles soak up the fun and the words 'wish you were here' are printed along the top. This is what I hold up. The seaside looks so much fun! I want to go! I must go! So my escape begins.

I wriggle and wriggle, trying desperately to be free from this notice board of memories. I fall on my back with my point facing upwards. Suddenly a huge, pink flip-flop edges closer and closer and then . . . *argh!* How will I get there now? Wherever this flip-flop goes, I will go! *Flip-flop, flip-flop*, we're on the move.

I'm now in a large space and I think, yes, I'm moving. We must be on wheels. A car? Yes, it must be! I'm not alone. There is a brightly coloured, large ball and a large castle, made of plastic? We've stopped.

Flip-flop, flip-flop. The texture of the ground has now changed. It's now warm and soft. I can hear laughing and splashing. The noise is overwhelming! But I can feel myself coming loose from the flip-flop. I drop off. I can now see everything I saw on the postcard! I now lie in the white sand soaking up the fun! Wish you were here!

Love Pin.

Esther Fee (13)
St Bede's RC High School, Blackburn

Rendezvous

The car engine stopped, and all was silent. The rain lashed onto the car windscreen and the thunder cracked loudly in the cloudy, grey sky. She looked at the rolled up piece of paper that had been pushed through her letterbox that morning. Slowly, she uncurled the note, squinting at the scruffy handwriting, smudged by the rain. Her stomach churned when she re-read the blotchy ink that told her: 'Meet me inside the old, abandoned house at exactly eight o'clock tonight'. She looked at her watch, only two more minutes left.

She glanced at the old, ramshackle building looming ahead of her. The wind was furious, making the car sway from side to side. A wave of nausea hit her, rocking her to the core. She looked in her wing mirror and tidied up her beautiful, long, golden hair. Her rosy cheeks glowed in the moonlight and her beautiful blue eyes twinkled like the stars.

She pulled the handle of the car door and pushed it open. She swung her legs to the edge of her seat and zipped up her coat. The ferocious wind hit the side of the door, sending it slamming into her thin frame. Her legs, trapped in the door, sent a rush of panic down her spine. Shivering, she regained her composure and tried again, managing to free her body from the car.

She stepped into the icy chill of the wind, her hair blowing around her face. The path to the house was uneven, with a light layer of gravel that crunched underfoot. The rain lashed down on her like a thousand knives. Clutching the note in her clammy palms, she made her way to the rundown house. Her heart was racing as she scrabbled for the door handle . . .

Kaitlin King (13)
St Bede's RC High School, Blackburn

A Day In The Life Of A Butterfly

The moonlight shines down upon the whispering wilderness, delicately caressing the woodland as it gently arouses the innocent inhabitants from their dreary slumber. Reluctant and unaware, mesmerised by the outstretching dawn, the creatures of the night retreat, alas, to their domain, surrounded by the enchanting pitter-patter of the morning dew settling upon the forest floor. All darkness soon withdrawn from the brightening day, the woodland is once again alive with the sound of freedom - up in the trees, along the sea of torrenting leaves dancing with the bliss morning breeze and down by the prominent pond at the heart of the forest.

Valiant in its sensational beauty, the butterfly reaches out with its kindred wings, aspiring for the warmth and solace of the beaming sunlight through the passing mist. The chrysalis hang, as though raindrops of beauty, untouched by nature, each one unique as a symbol of metamorphosis. The butterfly guards them by night, by day. Taking flight, it beats its fabulous cloak of colours, swiftly darting through the wild lands, gone in a flash, never to be seen until caught on the final resting day, gradual in pace with solemn grace and class.

The mother of nature, the eye of all beauty, the unfading rainbow of creatures and insects alike, the symbol of elegance . . . the butterfly.

Carly Baldwin (12)
St Bede's RC High School, Blackburn

Mobile Phones - Good Or Bad?

This week there has been more anxiety over the safety of mobile phones after a boy was viciously murdered for his phone.

In this discussion, we look at the arguments over how vulnerable mobile phone users actually are. Some say we are putting our lives in jeopardy, while others would strongly disagree.

People who believe that mobile phones are a good thing say that if a child has a mobile, their parents can be more relaxed, knowing that the child is safe. However, as the recent murder has proved, people carrying mobile phones run the risk of being mugged.

Parents pay a lot of money to top up their children's phones, yet almost all the children we questioned said that they are given a certain amount each month, if they go over that, they have to pay for another top up themselves or wait until the next month to get another one.

Scientists believe that constant use of a mobile can lead to brain damage, but this has never been proven.

In a recent survey we carried out, we found out that over 90% of people had a mobile phone, and that nearly 95% of people believed that mobile phones were safe.

In conclusion, despite recent happenings, mobile phones are relatively safe, but anybody carrying a mobile phone should be aware of the risks!

Marc Brennan (13)
St Bede's RC High School, Blackburn

A Day In The Life Of A Penguin!

Documentary presenter stood approximately twenty metres away: 'The penguin: arguably one of the most fascinating birds on the planet. Capable of outrunning a fully grown man if it has to, which is strange considering its usual waddling speed is only a steady three kilometres an hour. Watch it as it turns to face us; we can only wonder what, if anything, it is thinking.'

'Why are all those people looking at me?' pondered Percy. 'All I want to do is stand here in peace.' He was feeling quite down, because his partner hadn't come back. She'd gone on her usual holiday with all the other females, which wouldn't normally have bothered him in the slightest, but most of his mates' partners had come back about a week ago. He wanted her to come back soon because he missed her, as well as being fed up with standing with that stupid egg balanced on his feet day and night. 'They're probably filming another of those documentaries that the senior penguins are always talking about.'

'The name 'penguin' originally comes from the Welsh 'pen' meaning head and 'gywn' meaning white. Oh look; here comes a female, back from her annual vacation.'

Finally, thought Percy, *here comes Polly.*

As soon as he had passed the egg over to her, he slid down the hill to the sea. He went soaring off the lip at the end of the ice. It felt wonderful to be free again, almost as if he was flying. He shot into the water at tremendous speed and shivered, he had forgotten just how freezing, yet refreshing, the water was.

Chris Burt (13)
St Bede's RC High School, Blackburn

No More Tears

Amy liked funerals, she always had. Ever since she was a toddler, she had such vivid memories of going to church with her mum. Her older sister, Louise, thought she was mad. 'It's boring,' she always said. But Amy didn't care because for her, churches were magical places. She loved the smell of polished wood and how there was always a dazzling array of flowers. Often the sunlight poured through the stained glass windows, sending colours dancing along the walls. Amy always took delight in snuggling up to her mum. It was her one precious hour of the week where she had her all to herself. No jobs, no phones with their insistent ring. Most of all, church offered Amy a chance to talk to her dad.

Amy's father died shortly after she was born. Her memories of him were a few precious photographs. She managed to keep his memory alive by lighting a candle each week, but it was at funerals where she felt most connected to him.

Today's funeral had brought out all the family. Mum often said that weddings and funerals were the only time this family got together. Amy looked at all the sad faces and wanted to say to them all, 'No more tears.' She tried to snuggle up to her mum, but she was wrapped in her own grief.

Then she heard her dad calling her. 'Amy, it's time to go.'

'I know, Dad,' she replied softly, 'I just wanted to say goodbye.'

Amy glanced one last time at the beautiful white coffin with her name etched in the polished gold plate. *Yes,* thought Amy, *I love funerals . . . even mine,* as she took her father's hand.

Sarah Cooper (12)
St Bede's RC High School, Blackburn

A Day In The Life Of An Escaped Convict

Pant, pant, pant! I was running out of breath. *Tap, tap, tap!* The footsteps behind me grew louder.

'Got to keep going, got to keep going,' I murmured to myself over and over again, as I knew the guard was catching up with me and I knew that if he caught up with me, I would never see daylight again.

A dark alleyway was getting nearer, the perfect place to lead my victim to his death. At least it would get the police off my back for a few days.

I walked away feeling like a huge weight had been lifted off my back, but I still had to work out where I could run to next!

I walked and walked for miles on end, until I finally came across a small, dimly lit village. I hoped no one had seen my face plastered over their television, but that was a chance I had to take for I was cold, wet, tired and lonely. I took a chance to steal a glance into a small cottage and saw a happy family cuddled together on a sofa watching a Disney film. I saw this and I had never felt more alone!

I saw a nearby field and decided to stay there for a while and plan what I was going to do next and how I would do it.

Voices. I could hear voices. Getting closer. The muffled talking now became clear and what I heard sent an icy chill up my spine.

'She was seen here last night walking into this village, I'm afraid,' a polite voice was saying.

I scrambled to my feet and dived into a nearby bush. I trembled as the pain from the scratching, squeaking twigs dug into me. I could now see two men looking for something, or maybe someone!

I waited and waited for what seemed like hours until the men had gone, but in fact it was only half an hour. My stomach growled from hunger and my eyes drooped from exhaustion. There was no way I could live every day like this or I would be dead by the end of the week. Well, maybe I would be anyway.

When I finally reached a town, it was night. I decided to check into an hotel with the remaining money I had. I used a fake name and then went to find my room.

Fumbling with the key, I managed to open the door and I collapsed, falling asleep on the cheap and scratchy bed.

A few hours later I was awoken by loud thudding on the door. I pulled it open, still half asleep, but suddenly I jerked into reality when a pair of handcuffs were forced around my wrists and I was bundled into a police car . . .

Ruth Hartley (13)
St Bede's RC High School, Blackburn

A Day In The Life Of An Actress

I was in my jet early in the morning flying to my luxury apartment in LA where the awards ceremony was being held. I was up for an award! I arrived around 9.30am and as I stepped off my jet, there were my bodyguards, the paparazzi and my limousine!

When I got to my apartment, my beauticians were ready. I needed to look my best. I had my nails and hair done and a facial. After hours of pampering they were finished. I went out shopping for the finishing touches to my outfit.

After hours of shopping I bought a Gucci handbag, a pair of Manolo Blanhik shoes and a diamond necklace. On the way back to my apartment, I signed some autographs and carried on back home.

I had to get ready quickly when I got there. I was wearing a pale pink dress with diamond detailing on the front, a split up one side and a short train. My limousine was waiting outside for me. As I arrived, hundreds of people were making their way inside. I stepped onto the red carpet and a rush of excitement came over me!

In the hall I could see familiar faces wishing each other the best, but hoping they would win really. It got to my award, I was nervous.

'And the winner of Best Actress is . . .'

I suddenly went into a daze! But then people began clapping and pointing to me. I had won! I stood up, still unsure, I said my speech, thanking everyone for their support and sat back down shaking.

After the awards there was a party, which I went to and I didn't arrive home until early in the morning. I sank into my four-poster bed. I was exhausted! What a hectic job.

Rebecca McCann (13)
St Bede's RC High School, Blackburn

Clare's Fables
(With apologies to Aesop)

The racehorse and the donkey:

A racehorse once ridiculed the huge ears and long face of a donkey. But the donkey gave a sweet little giggle and replied, 'Although you may gallop like lightning, I'll still beat you in a flat race!'

'Alright,' said the racehorse arrogantly, 'you will regret saying those words!

So they both came to an agreement that the zebra would choose the racecourse and fix the finishing line.

On the day set for the race, the donkey started plodding at his usual steady pace without stopping for a nibble of a nearby pile of carrots. Of course, the racehorse left the donkey way behind at the first furlong. Once he reached the midway point, he began to nibble on some long, juicy grass. Since the day was long and warm, he decided to take a little nap in a shady spot. Even though the donkey might pass him while he slept, he was very confident that he could overtake him to win the race.

Meanwhile, the unwavering donkey plodded on straight towards the goal.

When the racehorse finally awoke, he was amazed to find that the donkey was nowhere to be seen and headed for the finish line as fast as he could. Unfortunately, he rushed across the finishing line only to see that the donkey had crossed it before him and the donkey was comfortably resting and waiting for his arrival.

Overconfident and cocky loses the race.

Clare Edwards (13)
St Bede's RC High School, Blackburn

A Day In The Life Of A Pair Of Shoes

I am sitting here at the door. It's really cold here. I hear footsteps. Banging, something crashing. Water running. Doors opening. People talking. Someone's coming, closer and closer. I can see them! They're coming closer and closer, closer than ever before. I'm being picked up, someone's squeezing into me. I'm going out into the rain, to begin my day as a shoe.

I'm getting wet! My beautiful, glossy shine is going, going, gone. Oh no! I'm getting filthy! My owner is running through puddles, muddy puddles! I'm wet through! The soles of me are worn in. The water's seeping through me! It's horrible!

I can smell something. It smells musty, like rotting socks! It's disgusting! It smells like my owner's socks haven't been washed since they were put on. Weeks ago! The mud is making them smell even worse! The shoes around me all look so happy. Their owners all make them so happy, mine makes me unhappy. Surely they could have a wash once in a while!

Wait. One minute. Something's happening. The rain's stopping. The sun's coming out! Yes! I love the sun. It makes me smile. It's so happy. The puddles are disappearing! I'm drying, but oh no! the mud's drying on! You can hardly see the black of my shoes! It was only this morning when I was all black and shiny with added gloss. Oh no, this day can't get any worse!

Oh no, oh no! My owner is walking right towards some dog poo! They've walked right into it! So now, I don't only have an owner with smelly feet, my shoe is full of mud, but now I have dog poo all over the sole of my shoe!

My owner is walking towards a bin. They've taken me off and now I'm in the bin, gone forever.

Gabrielle Wilson (12)
St Bede's RC High School, Blackburn

It

Your voice echoes throughout the empty house, your breath icy as the night, clouds of smoke emerge from your mouth. Cold. Dark.
Damp.
Ring, ring . . .
Ring, ring . . .
You jolt upright, your heart racing on a treadmill. Towards the phone you trudge, the echoes ebbing away.
Ring, ring . . .
You pick up the receiver and cautiously bring it to your ear; breathing, deep breathing. You break the silence, 'H-hello?' A voice, but not quite scary, the plumber in fact!
'Oh hiya, the heating went off earlier due to some complications!'
'Oh thanks,' your voice, dull, flat though relieved.
You let your tense muscles flex and relax and sit on the moth-eaten couch, close your eyes and listen to the night. Silent . . .
Images run through your mind, you can't focus, noise, blur, pounding, pounding, noise, blur, pounding, pounding, *silence* . . .
Crystal shivers slither up your spine, through your body. The moonlight catches your eye through the window. Intrigued, you stop, stare . . .
. . . A silhouette, black, tall, lanky, lurking, looking, morphing? You stand, transfixed upon the figure which is pouring through the cracks of the windowpane, not liquid, not solid, not anything. As it lands on the floor, it rebuilds to its original form with eyes, piercing eyes, glaring eyes, familiar eyes, your eyes.
You stay screwed to the spot, so does 'it'. You make a dash for the stairs, heart in throat, though slip. You frantically scan the house for 'it', though no trace, nothing.
Never again did you stay alone.

Stephanie Hargreaves (13)
St Bede's RC High School, Blackburn

Conflict Desert Storm III

The four soldiers dived into the ditch and lay prone. Immediately, several Republican Guards came rushing at them with light machine guns. The four soldiers covered the specially converted Puma helicopter that had deployed them. It got away safely and then the shoot-out began. Soon the Republican Guards were dead where they lay. These skilled soldiers were Britain's SAS and they were: John Bradley, rifleman and team leader, Paul Foley, sniper, Mick Connors, heavy weapons specialist and Dave Jones, demolitions expert and combat engineer. Their mission was to infiltrate Saddam Hussein's barracks in Baghdad and assassinate him, therefore ending Operation Desert Storm III and the third Gulf War.

Cautiously, the squad advanced. They saw a SCUD missile launcher.

'Jones, take it out with a frag grenade,' Bradley whispered.

'Right.' Jones pulled out of his inventory a 40mm fragmentation grenade. 'This should do it.' He aimed and it was a direct hit.

The barracks were now in sight. The squad were expecting heavy defence, so crawled forwards. Their guess was correct.

'Connors, you could take most of the guards out with your LAW-66, couldn't you?' Bradley whispered.

'Aye.' Connors pulled out his anti-tank missile. He had two shots.

Foley took out the surviving guards with his sniper as they were at long range. They ran down to the complex and shot down the door. They were in.

It was huge inside. There was another door at the end of the hall. It had 30mm armour, so Bradley told Jones to blast it with another 40mm frag grenade. Bradley was in front, so took out the guards at the door to the chambers of Saddam Hussein with his M16A2 assault rifle.

He was lying on his bed with guards surrounding him. However, the team were expecting this and Connors threw in two smoke grenades. They went in and blindly shot everywhere. Then the gas cleared. The guards were dead and Saddam Hussein was on his knees. He was begging for mercy. Bradley stepped forward and slit Hussein's throat. They then ran out. Foley took down the guards from through the doors.

There, waiting for them, protected by four Apache helicopters, was their Puma. Mission complete.

Chris Hughes (13)
St Bede's RC High School, Blackburn

Drosnin's Deception?
The Bible Code Revelation!

Is the forthcoming book 'The Bible Code III' written by reporter Michael Drosnin, viable in the eyes of reason? This is the question the reporting community asks itself; in a time when the Middle East has renewed hatred for the West and an increasingly violent atmosphere.

The two 'Bible Code' books written by the former 'Wall Street Journal' reporter, describe the discovery of a 3000-year-old code, in the first five books of the Bible, that predicts events in the future, including September 11th.

I have personally read Drosnin's latest book 'The Bible Code II' and found myself becoming embroiled in a way I find unnatural as a reporter.

Perhaps this is due to the large amount of statistical evidence and, in my opinion, its slightly apocalyptic nature.

Not surprisingly, sceptics and scientists have examined Drosnin's findings, arriving at some quite embarrassing conclusions.

The code-finding method used by Drosnin, is heavily based on that of Dr Eliyahu Rips, a leading mathematical expert.

A computer searches for selected names or words, by jumping so many characters, to find each letter. One of Drosnin's most referred to predictions, is the assassination of Yitzhak Rabin, the former Israeli prime minister. This prediction uses jumps of 4,772 characters!

Sceptics argue that simple groups of relevant words, can be found easily in most texts.

For example, 'Hitler' and 'Nazi' can be found in Tolstoy's 'War and Peace', a modern classic.

Dr Eliyahu Rips also denies working jointly with Drosnin; although at first blush, the books seem to imply the opposite. Dr Rips also stated that he does not support Drosnin's work, or conclusions.

The truth remains uncertain.

Chris Sharples (13)
St Bede's RC High School, Blackburn

A Stars Myth

Once upon a dark time, when only gods roamed the quiet planet, a god called Aquma noticed how lonely and deserted the Earth was. He decided to hold a meeting with the other gods about what they should do. After four hours of discussion, they came up with the idea of making another creature. This creature was to have two legs, two arms, five fingers, a head, a face, two eyes and a mouth. It was to worship the gods and be called 'man'.

The gods worked hard on their new project for a week, until man was made. They gave man life and placed it on Earth. The gods were very satisfied with their new creation and made lots more. The only thing bad about them was that they didn't look up to the gods or thank them for being created, which made the gods very angry. Instead, they fought and argued and complained at what little they had.

The gods thought about this and decided to punish man if they complained, argued or fought against each other once more. Man heard about this and stopped complaining about life. But then they started fighting at night when the gods were asleep, instead of during the day.

One night, Aquma was up fishing. He overheard man at war with each other.

The next day he was furious and told the other gods. Aquma wanted something done and had an idea. He was to create spies that would keep an eye on man overnight and tell Aquma if anything happened.

So he set to work and made white, shiny spots called stars, that would hang in the sky at night. Aquma made the moon, a larger yellow ball, to govern the stars that would govern the selfish beings on Earth.

At last everyone was happy and after a while, man started to not fight, became grateful to the gods and began to appreciate their lives.

This system worked for 1,000 centuries and still works today. So always remember not to fight or complain about life, just think of what will happen to you if you do!

Dominic Marshall (12)
St Bede's RC High School, Blackburn

The Creation Of The Stars

After man and all the creatures had been created, Calambi, their creator, hoped that everyone would live together in peace and harmony. But he was wrong, very wrong.

There were two rival cities that didn't like each other one tiny bit. They would argue and fight about little things, instead of trying to befriend one another and sort the major problems. But both cities, just on their border, were separated by a vast desert spreading for mile upon mile with no sign of life whatsoever. A barren wasteland. In the middle of this desert was a mine, but it wasn't just any old mine. Inside it hid beautiful treasures that were worth more than money could buy. There was just one problem. Both cities owned the land, therefore they could dig for the gems. So both cities gathered up an army of miners to dig and soldiers to defend the miners.

After many days of travelling, both groups finally reached the mine, but seconds later, they spotted each other. Both armies charged, starting a major battle. The miners began digging for the gems.

This made Calambi very angry, but he decided not to do anything to see if they could sort out their problem by themselves.

So the battle carried on for a number of weeks. Soldiers died, but were replaced and miners were trapped, but were also replaced. The number of precious gems soon piled up for each city, until most of them had been dug out.

Finally, Calambi decided to take action because the battle hadn't sorted itself out. To punish the people, he decided to send down a tornado, to destroy everyone and everything, including the gems, in its path. The people fled for their lives, but soon their greediness took over. They ran for the gems, but the tornado just swallowed them up.

Soon everyone had gone. There was nothing left.

Later, both mayors decided to put their bad past behind them and become good friends. But they began to wonder where all their civilians had gone. But on a clear night, when they were out talking, they looked up at the night sky to see white splodges, shimmering. Then they realized that they were the gems. They had been displayed for all to see.

Chris Metz (12)
St Bede's RC High School, Blackburn

How The Stars Came To Be

As the sun was rising, the goddess Shelah was slowly opening her black velvet curtains from the sky above. She gazed at a land that was green, rich and plentiful with fruit and honey. The deep, warm, crystal clear sea held tureens of fish and other weird and wonderful creatures. That was the land which the goddess created, although she missed one important feature in her humans - kindness.

One day she decided to test her humans and see if they really were unkind and horrible. So after much debating with the other gods, she came to a conclusion. She was to give her humans a sart. (A sart is a small, pure, silver cup, which is extremely delicate and fragile.)

'Greetings my friends,' she cried, 'as a gift from your gorgeous goddess Shelah, I give you this sart.'

Eyes opened wide and mouths opened too, even a few people fainted! Shelah curtsied and disappeared in the blink of an eye.

'Look at my lovely sart!' shouted one.

'I know! Isn't my sart beautiful? Look at that . . .' said another excited with the thought of his own sart.

'Excuse me! Pardon me! Isn't that sart mine?' puzzled one human.

'No, it is mine! For I am the cleverest!' stated another.

The arguments went on and on until nightfall, with everybody arguing their case on why they should have the sart. Would the arguments ever stop?

'Right!' screamed an elderly man. 'I'm keeping the sart until we can decide who is having the silver cup.' With that he grabbed the cup.

'No, it's OK, I shall keep the cup, for I am more responsible than you lot!' Then he grabbed and pulled the cup with full force.

The startled old man held on with fury and anger. Arguments broke out again while the other humans were fighting.

Crack! The cup broke into a million pieces and flew up into the dark, velvet sky. Silver pieces streamed up in the cold night air and stopped there. The humans were puzzled. Why weren't the pieces falling down? So they went to sleep troubled and distressed.

In the morning, Shelah came to their village settlement and said, 'As you broke the cup last night, my trust in you has gone. In the sart's place I have put the stars. They shall remain in the night sky and shall remind you and others of your wickedness and unkindness. From now onwards, every time you do a good deed for someone you do not like, a star shall fall. It shall be called a shooting star. When you have all done a good deed, you will have your sart back. Until that day, goodbye.'

As she said, until that day, Shelah's people are still trying to do good deeds, for it is their fate to collect stars.

Danielle Moore (12)
St Bede's RC High School, Blackburn

The Creation Of The Stars

In South America, a man named Claudio was vicious to animals, he chopped down trees, he disturbed habitats, he poisoned plants and he killed flowers. After many years of Claudio doing these cruel and selfish acts, the gods grew so angry, they were breathing flames.

One clear and crisp morning in the middle of summer, all of the people in South America awoke to see that all the lush green grass was brown, all the multicoloured flowers were droopy and colourless. All the healthy green leaves on the trees were lifeless and brown. However, Claudio couldn't care less. He preferred it to be dull and dismal.

That night, when Claudio was sleeping soundly, the furious god, Sun, appeared in his dreams.

'Claudio, you are an extremely mean person. Therefore, you leave me and all the other gods no choice but to banish you from this Earth, to prevent you from doing any more damage to nature and life!' the outraged god exclaimed.

The gods performed exactly what Sun said they would and not one single thing lay on Claudio's bed.

That morning everything was back to normal. The people of South America were filled with joy and happiness!

Two nights later, the god, Moon, rose and spoke to South America and the rest of the world.

'Every night from now on, I will be accompanied by 5-pointed stars that will shine brightly in the night sky. They will represent the five terrible things that Claudio did to nature and life!'

From that point up to today, the moon and the 5-pointed stars shine brightly in the velvety night sky.

Bianca Castela (12)
St Bede's RC High School, Blackburn

Untitled

I'll never forget the night, that cold, dark, grisly night of the 12th November; the horrific date on which my very own life was somehow snatched and seized . . . forever.

A cold breeze swirled, making the trees whisper, as dead leaves scuttled around my legs and crackled beneath my shoes as I, Michael Rowswell, padded towards my house. A cold chill trickled down my back as I heard a sound echo in the soft whisper of the wind, and there stood a dark, sinister figure, covered in a long, black cloak. I began to run, my arms thrashing wildly, my heart pounding. I passed the woods and scampered to my room as I panted. I clicked the light switch, but it refused to work. Suddenly, a shadow appeared in front of me. It moved closer, pulsing up the wall and it was there, just there. My entire body was gripped with terror. I tried to scream, but only a low groan escaped my throat. I braced myself as the eerie figure lurched forward and ferociously attacked me. Who was this? What did it want? These questions pounded relentlessly, slapping me, demanding an answer as I squirmed helplessly. And then it happened . . . it replaced my life.

I felt a tingling sensation and from me came a bellow of rage, so despairing, so filled with anguish and torment, that every creature within hearing distance shivered with fear. Animals hid in burrows and trees and people in their houses slid deeper beneath their bed covers, taking refuge from the obscene sound. And only the wildest of forest creatures continued to hear the echo of the tortured wail in the soft whisper of the wind.

Simeon Adeoye (12)
St Bede's RC High School, Blackburn

Santa Claus Gets The Sack (And Some Leftover Presents Too!)

Today's young generation are wishing away Santa and his sacks full of presents

The recent surveys that have been carried out in random towns and cities have suggested that today's youngsters of Britain are losing their faith in Santa Claus much earlier than ever before.

For young children all over the world, Christmas is one of the most exciting events of the year. The captivating Father Christmas has enchanted the minds and hearts of toddlers and primary school girls and boys. But when one has older children to think about, it is hard for a parent to tell one child the truth of Santa Claus and keep it secret from the other. A similar survey carried out 7 years ago, confirmed that between the ages of 9-13 was the time in which children heard about the man who lived with elves at the North Pole didn't actually exist.

Parents and citizens are now beginning to wonder whether or not the make-believe Santa Claus story will proceed through the first ten years of their children's lives. One slip of the tongue that might prove Father Christmas' non-existence, could question a child's mind forever.

Experts believe that within 10-20 years, children will find out how Father Christmas isn't real as easily as they find out the fairy tale of how he was; and that this could happen at an age as young as four or five. They also fear that parents will take this for granted and will eventually not bother to tell the tale of the old man who rides a sleigh through the sky on Christmas Eve.

So will this be the extinction of Santa Claus? And if so, will Christmas ever be known as the family day full of season's greetings? Only time will tell.

Emily Davison (13)
St Bede's RC High School, Blackburn

A Day In The Life Of A Goldfish

Ouch! That hurt. Why is there a wall that I can't see? It's confusing. There's two of us here. Me and Josh. There used to be more of us I think, but they all died. Oh, I can't remember - the stress, it's too much!

'The stress of anything is too much for your tiny brain.'

That was Josh, he's always nasty to me. I hate him. I want to kill him! Oh my God, what did I just say? No, really I've forgotten. It was something about Josh. Oh well, forget it. Ouch! That hurt! Why is there a wall that I can't see? It's confusing. I'm feeling déjà-vu. Have I said that before?

'Idiot.'

I wish Josh would stop muttering. What did he say? I've forgotten.

'I said, idiot. I was talking about you.'

That was Josh. He's always nasty to me. I want to kill him! Get here, you evil flapper! Call yourself a goldfish? Got you! How shall I kill him? I know, I'll suffocate him - hold my fins over his gills so he can't breathe.

'Let go . . . get off . . .'

He's dead! Oh no, Josh is dead! And I'm holding him! Just like when the others died. They - I remembered something! Erm, what did I remember again? Oh well, no matter.

Ewww! Why have I got a dead fish in my fins? Eww, let go. I shall have a minute's silence in respect for the dead fish.

OK, I'm bored now. I can't even remember why I was being so quiet. Is the cat there? No. Is that big person home? No. So why am I being so quiet? Oh well, never mind. I'll do my exercises. Left, right, stretch down, stretch up. Oh God! What's that floating at the top? Is it . . . ? No, it can't be. Yes, it is - it's Josh! And he's - he's dead! Who killed him? Who killed Josh? Curse the villain who put an end to Josh's life! What did he do to deserve this? Oh Josh, my poor friend! My poor dead friend! Who killed him? I'll kill the nasty thing who put an end to Josh! I'll kill them.

Laura Summerfield (13)
St Bede's RC High School, Blackburn

The Black Knight

One stormy night, the wind was smashing up against the window, leaves swirled around, rain gushed down like the god of Earth, Earthina, was here, her anger all around.

In one particular house being lashed by the storm, a tiny, spiky-haired, talented boy slept. The trees started banging against the window and a microscopic man came through the glass, dressed in nothing but a torn piece of cloth.

In the morning, Jim woke up with a start, yelling that he had seen a little man setting up an Action Man camp. Jim bent down, thinking to himself, *what the monkey is that*?

Jim stared and said, 'What do you want?' The little man replied, 'I have come to do no harm, my people need you to help them.'

Jim said to the man, 'Nobody wants my help because all I do is lie about the vicious Black Knight.'

'Who?' said the little man in amazement.

Jim replied with a lie, 'The one ready to kill the wee free men.'

The man said, 'Is he the one you shout about in the night?'

'Yes,' said Jim quietly.

Months and days went by and the little people were happy because Jim had stopped shouting. Then, suddenly, one night whilst Jim was fast asleep, there was an unusual storm and a strange fog covered the roads all around. Then out of thin air came a man, a man dressed in black, riding on a horse, galloping through and tearing the fog apart like paper.

The little man whispered to Jim, 'He's here, the Black Knight is here.'

Jim slept through the night, not waking when the little man spoke.

In the morning he woke up suddenly. He looked out of the window and what he saw made him gasp in horror. He stood still and silent. It looked like a bomb site! Jim knew that only the Black Knight could do this. The little man told Jim he must warn people, so he bellowed to anyone who would listen, 'The Black Knight is here!'

People suddenly began to believe Jim and the next night, half of the town had fled. Jim went to bed and was soon in a restless sleep. The door slammed and Jim woke, fearing for himself. He fled and then stopped. He decided to put an end to the reign of the Black Knight.

Five weeks went by and Jim was to meet his destiny. Would he have a painful, gory death, or be showered in praise by the people who asked for his help?

The Black Knight was there. He hit Jim who fell to the ground with a thud and a blood-curdling howl. As he fell, he bellowed, 'It's the Black Knight.'

The end was near and Jim was lowered into the ground.

That night a terrible storm broke out and everyone heard something come galloping through the town. In a particular house, a little man began to set up camp.

Thomas Miller (11)
St Bede's RC High School, Blackburn

Tropical Love

Far, far away, there was an island with palm trees that swayed in the breeze, a deep blue sea and soft, silky sand. The sun shone on the island - it was gorgeous.

On this island there lived a princess. She was called Jamelia. Her hair was long and brown. It was as soft as a teddy bear. Her eyes were hazel-brown and they sparkled in the sun. The secret about this princess was that she could not escape this island until she found her prince.

Every day she would go on her cruise ship and wait for her prince. Every day was long and boring, just waiting and waiting.

One day she hopped onto her ship and the captain drove her around the water.

'What about him?' the captain asked.

'Well let me have a look,' she replied.

So the captain picked up the boy and he climbed onto the boat.

When he got onto the boat, it was love at first sight. She fell into his arms and they kissed.

'What is your name?' she asked.

'Anthony,' he said. 'I am the prince of this island.'

They came off the boat and walked along the shore. While they were walking, Anthony got down on one knee and proposed.

'I have been waiting for you forever, so will you marry me?' he asked.

'Yes, of course I will,' Jamelia said.

They carried on walking until they got to Jamelia's apartment. Jamelia then rang her father to tell him the good news. Her mother and father were very happy for them.

After a few months, the big day finally came and all Jamelia's and Anthony's families were there. They got married in the sunset, it was beautiful.

Bethany Weall (11)
St Bede's RC High School, Blackburn

The House On The Hill

As Grandpa Joe sat in his old, rusty chair, he smoked his wooden pipe, but was crying very loudly. One of his grandchildren entered the room. Her name was Mary. Mary was a tall girl, slim and pale. Her hair was red as flames, burning all day and night and her eyes were blue and green, making the colours of the sea's waves crashing upon a shore. A pleated dress she wore, beautiful and blue.

Then Tom, her younger brother, followed her in. Tom was a round boy and short, with hair as black as night.

'Hello, Grampa. Grampa, why are you crying?' said Mary, puzzled.
'Yes, what is the matter?' added Tom.
'Nothing,' sobbed Grandpa.
'Please,' pleaded Tom.

'Well, 49 years ago, me and your Grandma Rose were in the fields and an old woman fell out of a tree. *Argh!* she screeched, *get out of my field! This is my land and to walk on this land you will give me a helper, also you may go in the tree and there is gold. You will be rich beyond your wildest dreams!* she said. Never, I don't know any, I replied. Then Rose disappeared and came back in a cage with bars as thick as logs. Then they disappeared and I've not seen her since.'

Christina Hamill (12)
St Bede's RC High School, Blackburn

Book Review - 'Wuthering Heights'

(Abridged by Mary Calvert)

'Instead of grabbing a branch, my fingers closed round the fingers of an ice-cold hand. An intense horror came over me. I tried to bring back my arm but the hand clung to me, and the sad voice sobbed . . .'

Although this thrilling passage may come across as a spine-chilling, nail-biting, teeth-clenching horror story, as you dig deeper inside you will discover the harrowing happenings, the tragic traumas and the many mixed emotions of this breathtaking classic novel, 'Wuthering Heights'. Your bottom will practically be cemented into your chair and your eyes will be sealed within every page and every chapter of 'Wuthering Heights' as you read on to encounter the feelings of the perfidious yet infatuated Heathcliff!

'Wuthering Heights' was written by Emily Brontë in 1846. Brontë grew up in a large village on the edge of the Yorkshire moors, along with her father, her brothers and her sisters. From being the sweet and innocent age of two, Emily Brontë had an addictive affection for the mysterious moors. Brontë almost had the characteristics of the Yorkshire moors: lonely, silent and secretive.

Being the person she was, Brontë poured out her own concealed feelings onto every page of 'Wuthering Heights', making the novel compelling to read. Emily Brontë had longed for a passionate, dark and handsome lover to come along and whisk her away from the sheltered life that she lived. To Emily Brontë, Heathcliff was her quintessential lover. Writing 'Wuthering Heights' let Brontë break free from her solitary home life.

From the very beginning, you will become engrossed in the hidden feelings which Catherine Linton and Heathcliff truly feel for one another. By marrying the delightful, reliable Edgar Linton, Catherine escaped from her one and only true love, Heathcliff.

Ellen Dean, who is the trustworthy, affable servant in the novel, narrates the story throughout, including every detail of the mind-bending agonies and the poignant emotions experienced by both families. Heathcliff's passion and sincere revenge brings agonizing death and tragedy to both families. Leaving behind the heart-rending tragedies and fervour, the book ends on a hopeful note, putting an end to the family feud.

From reading 'Wuthering Heights' personally, I discovered the true meaning of the novel and conceived every emotion of each character, including the second generation of Catherine Linton. Every scene within every chapter of the book painted a vivid picture in my mind, which led me to feel as though I was sitting in a room with Catherine, Heathcliff and Edgar. The more you read this tantalising novel, the more you become involved in the Earnshaw and the Linton family!

This time, it's out with the new and in with the old! Forget 'Hollyoaks', because 'Wuthering Heights' is the one to read. 'Wuthering Heights' screams out true passion and agony between two lovers in denial. Never mind those meaningless 'teenage' programmes, 'Wuthering Heights' is sure to have almost every lovesick teenager shedding a sympathetic tear for the asphyxiated love of Catherine and Heathcliff!

Brydie Kennedy (12)
St Bede's RC High School, Blackburn

Best Mates

I came home from school early today. A message had come over the school's loudspeaker system. 'Will Bill Watson please report to reception immediately'. I trundled off amid the gaze of my classmates, grinning to myself for being excused from the demon science teacher's lesson. The grin didn't last long. As soon as I saw my mum's face, I knew that something dreadful had happened. I just looked at her, puzzled. 'What's wrong?' I asked.

'It's Ben,' she replied. 'There's been an accident. He's . . .' Her voice trailed off at that point and she began to cry.

I remember feeling awkward, but not much else about what happened from there. Everything seemed such a blur.

The next thing I know I'm here, lying on my bed, thinking about Ben and the good times we had. The most noticeable thing about Ben was the colour of his hair. It was jet-black and so thick. Whenever Mum had trimmed it, we all used to laugh and say she needn't have bothered as it would be back to its normal, unruly self the next day.

We'd grown up together, Ben and me, and seemed to have shared so much. He was my best mate, as well as a member of my family. We loved going to the park. Ben especially loved football, if you can call it that. I used to roll about with laughter just watching him trying to control the ball, running round and round in circles. He was useless, but so funny. I'm laughing to myself now, just thinking about him. I don't care what anyone says, he's irreplaceable. There'll never be another dog like Ben.

Ryan O'Toole (13)
St Bede's RC High School, Blackburn

Untitled

Galloping, faster . . . faster . . . As I raced, my heart pounded, skipping every other beat. The trees around me were now flames that waved and danced throughout the sky. Instinct told me to run, but my heart told me to stay. My mother lay dead and my father was gone, he too had been guided by his instinct. My heart pounded as I remembered how my mother lay; cold, stiff and still. Run was what I had to do!

The morning came and my head was full of confusion. What must I do? Then I realised that this was the place that my father came to when he ran as foal. He had told me how terrified he had been as the forest fire destroyed his world. I must retrieve what is mine. I must find what I desire . . . happiness. Then I saw it! The hill of hope! That hill is my destiny, where my father stood and called for me.

Boom! Thud! I fled, not knowing where I was to go, not feeling any pain. Flashbacks; the hill, my mother, my father, and my world, gone, destroyed, forever. I heard the cry, the pain, the moan. Faster, faster . . . I galloped through the tough brambles and overgrown swamps. The cry I heard, the moan I heard . . . my father.

Swiftly, effortlessly, I ran, not feeling the pain. *Boom!* The last shot. Then silent. Soundless. Stillness. I stopped, halted, cut off from my worry. There I saw him. My father. Just as my mother lay; cold, stiff and still.

'Flee,' he muttered weakly. 'You must vanish.'

The case was closed and he spoke, 'It's the kindest way; to let him rest,' the vet said.

Gemma Coar (12)
St Bede's RC High School, Blackburn

The Witch And The Knight

Once upon a time there was a witch looking out of her window to see if anyone was passing by. She spotted a knight walking up the hill by her castle, so she went outside to talk to him.

'Why, hello there,' cackled the witch. 'What makes you come up here?'

'Well, I left my sword and shield here last time I was up, so I've come to collect them,' explained the knight.

'Oh well, please, do come inside for a spot of tea.'

'No thanks, I would not go into a spooky castle with a witch!' shouted the knight.

'Oh, but have you forgotten that witches have special powers?'

Immediately after the witch had said that, she zapped the knight into a cage in her castle. She then went over to the giant and whispered into his ear, 'I have got a knight in that cage over there for you.'

Immediately the giant jumped up from where he was sitting and marched over to the cage. 'He's not fat enough!' roared the giant.

The witch replied, 'Yes, well that's what I'm working on. We'll feed him up and serve him to you for supper.'

The giant marched back over to his wooden seat and sat on it.

'So, since you'll be staying here in my castle for the night, you might want some food,' said the witch.

'Yes, I want food now. Bring me some food!'

'My pleasure,' cackled the witch.

The witch then went out of the room to the kitchen and zapped in lots of fattening foods. After she had prepared them, she took them over to the knight, who ate them all. He kept demanding more food, because he didn't know the witch was planning to feed him to the giant.

A few hours later, he could barely fit in the cage, so the witch decided he was fat enough. She started to boil her big cauldron and tied the knight above it, ready to lower him in.

By this time the witch had started to lower the knight into the pot, when suddenly there was a big crash and a dragon flew in. He picked up the witch and the giant and threw them out of the window. The dragon got the knight off the rope and put him on his back. Then the dragon flew off back to the knight's castle. He was saved!

Erin Finn (12)
St Bede's RC High School, Blackburn

Sad Swamp

Years passed, every day, every night, the princess longed for a husband. She cried every hour as the tears ran down her cheeks and fell into the swamp of sadness below her. Many brave knights tried to free her from Dragon Castle, but none prevailed.

One cloudy morning, Princess Furn woke up, sat beside her window sill, still gazing out into the world. Then, far in the distance, she saw a knight. A smile appeared on her face.

'Dum, di, di, dum, dum, dum,' hummed the knight in his shining armour. It reflected beautifully on the gleaming lake beside him, but on the other side was the swamp. One big black blob was the hideous reflection that the swamp gave. Then the dragon rose out of the swamp. He had entered the jaws of death.

'Have you not heard the stories? If you trespass, I'll eat you in the most horrifying way.'

'Spare me. I walk to the town of Bela. Please, I will never come across again, I swear.'

The dragon grunted and sank beneath the grime.

That night was cold, very cold. Everything turned to ice. The beast was hungry, so he went to the town of Bela. It started to snow so much that he charged back to his swamp. With one great, giant leap, he jumped into the swamp, but it was frozen. The knight saw this and ran to help. He broke the ice with the booze he was drinking and the beast then sank beneath. Then he came back up and said, 'You have a heart of gold, my son, I thank you. So you can marry my princess as a token of my appreciation.'

So they lived happily ever after and they were given gold which they spent on a female dragon for Tom, the dragon, and had six wonderful baby dragons. But, of course, that's another story!

Megan Ellison (11)
St Bede's RC High School, Blackburn

The Reason The Stars And Sun Were Formed

Long ago, when the world was new, there were two large tribes, each worshipping two different gods.

At the beginning they both lived in harmony, none fought about land. There were no wars, until both tribes started to get greedy and wanted more land. At first, farmers would just have fights, with no serious injuries.

But then the gods forced them into war. The gods fought each other and the people fought each other. Every time a warrior died, a bright light would appear in the sky. The more loyal the warrior, the bigger the light. This light was a star.

The battle went on until one day a god died. A huge, bright, yellow and orange light appeared. This light was the sun.

James Walsh (11)
St Bede's RC High School, Blackburn

A Day In The Life Of A Goldfish

Living in a glass bowl is a constant dangerous sport for a fish, especially when you live with a cat. Occasionally, my existence becomes threatened by four evil paws, their claws and a clamping jaw with sharp teeth.

Each morning I read 'The Daily Fish' delivered by the postman and I often take a while to think about my family. My father was overfed and died from being bloated. My mother swam away with a pufferfish and left me stranded in the ocean until I was caught by a diver. Now I live in the Archibald residence and as the children thunder down the stairs, I watch the rockery in my bowl shake.

Reading my water bills which came in the mail, I put on my glasses and relax and I usually get a phone call from Grandmother Maureen checking if everything's OK. On Sundays, I cook her a roast and she comes with a packet of fish treats for my supper. She washes my working overalls. I'm a painter and decorator and she enjoys sitting in my armchair blowing bubbles to the surface.

On Tuesdays, I attend Book Club and discuss novels with other members of the group. This week we are reading, 'It's a Fish Life' by the famous author, Bubble Blower. (The meeting will be held in my bowl this week and so Grandmother Maureen is bringing some spare stools.)

I am currently searching for a new tank or an aquarium because my bowl is too small for a growing goldfish! The estate agent is paying me a visit tomorrow.

Gemma Barnes (12)
St Bede's RC High School, Blackburn

They're Here

From the corner of her eye, Rachael spotted an NHS 'Quit Smoking' sign. It reminded her of her best friend, Matilda. She loved spending time with here, in fact she was on the way to her house right now, but she really wished she didn't smoke. Every time Rachael left Matilda's house, she left stinking of smoke. Plus, Matilda's health was slowly deteriorating.

When she turned the corner, Rachael's face fell. Dark grey smoke wrapped around the house like a blanket. She began to run. A neighbour was talking to the fire brigade on his mobile. Faint screams came from the house. She must do something! Rachael picked up a spade and heaved it through the door. After a hard struggle, the door lifted free and Rachael stepped inside the blazing living room.

Matilda slowly crawled up the hallway. Her thoughts sped around her head like bees searching for honey. She had no strength. Sweat dripped down her nose. She could feel the hardened, singed carpet. Bright orange fire licked at her heels. The deafening crackle of flames surrounded her. Black smoke got in her eyes and mouth and left a very bitter taste. A peculiar and acrid scent filled her nostrils. Matilda struggled for breath. When would the fire brigade arrive? Her muscles relaxed and her eyelids began to droop. Suddenly, Matilda's ears pricked. She could hear sirens.

'They're here,' someone whispered.

Anna Jackson (12)
St Bede's RC High School, Blackburn

How The Sun, Moon, Stars, Day And Night Were Made

The old chief of the village was getting very old and very ill. The whole village sat around his sickbed to hear his last story and pray for him to go to Heaven. He was about to tell his village the last ever story he would tell. He chose the first one he'd ever heard. It was the one about the sun, the day and the night:

'It was all in the beginning when the world was just new. The people of the world were all in darkness. They complained because they wanted to sleep for half of the day, but wanted to stay awake for the other half. They could only sleep in this dark because they could not see what they were doing. The people of the world did not know what light was. Then suddenly, a small twinkle appeared in the sky. The people saw a man chasing after it. He was shouting, 'My jewel, my jewel!'

The people of the Earth learned that he had been greedy and Urethra, the god of the world, took away his jewels. Urethra called a meeting for the whole world to attend. She told them that if they were greedy and tried to take anyone else's jewels, they would lose all their jewels and they would come up as little lights in the sky called stars, and face the consequences. She used the greedy man as an example. 'You will suffer the consequences for being so greedy and you will not live as a human again. You will bring light into the world so people can sleep and work at the same time. You will be called the sun and you will be the brightest of all the stars. You will rule for 12 hours of the day, while I will rule for 12 hours at night.'

And so it was that the greedy man was made as the sun, shining bright. Some people of the world decided that at night it was not bright enough (because Urethra was modest, she did not make herself very bright), so they gave up some of their jewels to brighten it up more. Urethra decided that she would divide the Earth, so that when one half was light, the other half would be dark and then at 12 hours they would change.

Urethra put her hand on the Earth and made it spin slowly, so that when she was to rule the other side, it would very slowly change. This was called day and night. Urethra (moon) ruled the Earth at night and the greedy man (sun) ruled at day. Then Urethra drew a line around the Earth to separate the land from the sea.

That is how day, night, stars, sun and moon were made. Every night a new star appears in the sky. These are anyone who commits a crime.'

The chief gave a cough and fell asleep, never to awaken again.

Hayley McFarlane (11)
St Bede's RC High School, Blackburn

The Shadow King

As darkness falls across the land, the midnight hour is close at hand. A shadow ran like lightning through the long, striped grass.

Thirty men were guarding the king and his beautiful daughter. The thirty men were slaughtered like a knife through paper.

The king heard the terrible news and said, 'Send out your strongest men.'

So one hundred men ran out and guarded the wall. There was a black, horrible thing hiding in the corner. It jumped out and slaughtered them in seconds. The king heard their cries. Then a person walked by with long, black hair, with a sword, a bow and arrows on the other side. He bowed to the king. Then the monster jumped through the window and grabbed the king. The daughter came out of her room. The monster shot some fireballs at the daughter, but the soldier jumped in the way and put them out. He grabbed the monster's arm. The monster had never felt so much strength in a person.

'I will kill you if you touch him,' shouted the soldier.

'Kill me? No man has ever been able to kill me,' replied the monster.

'I am no man, you look upon a woman.'

The king gave her the castle, the money and the title of Queen.

James Balshaw (12)
St Bede's RC High School, Blackburn

A Day In The Life Of An Aborted Baby

The following story is a thought diary of a newly growing foetus baby and its heartbreaking fate at the end.

Monday:

I have finally finished my seventh week in my mother's stomach! It is strange, as I can finally see my surroundings. The walls are a soft, cushiony jelly, keeping my bright red skin warm. I am constantly hearing noises from outside my home - my mother crying (I think she is crying as she keeps yelping in small, long gulps) and a gruff voice is shouting. I think this is my father. It is rare that I hear his voice, as he is usually not around. I think this is why Mother cries. It is probably just her hormones though. I bet she is thrilled about having me. I imagine her to have flowing blonde curls with a smile that is heartwarming, like the sun. She should be quite tall, with sparkling blue gem eyes. I hope she is kind and will have a warm, powdery smell and soft hands like cotton wool when she holds me. But I would be just as happy if she is extremely ugly, as long as she will love me like I love her.

I hope my father has a sweet, humorous personality - not one that matches his tough voice. I would like him to be a teacher, or a helper with a charity. He should be gentle, with big, warm hands and floppy brown hair with hazel eyes. But, like I said, I am not fussed.

I am so excited! I wish I could break out of here right now, instead of waiting for nine long months! But I am not strong enough yet. Bits of my body are still shaping, like these long sausage shapes which hang near my head, and the other pair near my belly.

My mother was screaming again today. I heard a loud shout from my mother and two loud bangs on my surrounding wall. I am still confused as to what is wrong. It will be OK. It has to be. My dream is to have a perfect home, perfect parents and a perfect life. It might be a lot to ask for, but I will make it come true. Honest.

Tuesday:

Today, my mother killed me.

Jodie McNally (13)
St Bede's RC High School, Blackburn

How The Stars Got There!

A long, long time ago in a faraway, ancient land called Malio, lived thousands of butterflies, all colourful and bright. The butterflies lived alongside the people and gods of Malio. These butterflies were silver, gold, pink, yellow, green and blue. They made the island bright and shiny. People thought they were wonderful and so did a young man called Saul. Saul would sit outside on the lush green grass, just watching them twinkle all day long.

One day, Saul, decided to capture them and keep them for himself. He did for a few days.

When he could see no more around, he took them all to the top of Mount Aroma which carried a wonderful smell of flowers, lavender, tulips and lilies.

He built a shack for him and his butterflies, with no light. He did not need light for he had the butterflies to make everything glowing bright.

He did not notice Malio had gone dull. The people of Malio were no longer happy, but they were sad.

A few days later, the god of nature, Amoz, came to Saul and had a little word.

'Listen Saul, you need to set the butterflies free, for you have made Malio dull and unhappy. The butterflies are for *all* the people of Malio, not just for *you!*'

'But I love them so much. They make me happy and make me smile.'

'If you let them free, Saul, I promise you that they will be somewhere where you can enjoy them forever - not just you, everybody!'

That night, Amoz and the other gods went to the top of the mountain and helped Saul set the butterflies free. They fluttered into the night sky. It was a fantastic sight - the luminous colours covering the sky. They flew higher and higher until all you could see was a twinkle. Then the gods froze them and enjoyed them twinkling, looking beautiful. They are still there today, so we can enjoy them too.

Courtney Thomas (11)
St Bede's RC High School, Blackburn

The Story Of The Stars

A long time ago in Peru, a story was told about how the stars came about. The people of the world worshipped a great god called Joko. He was a mighty leader. Joko had built mountains and forests, constructed animals and rivers, and finally, he built his people houses.

One day Joko thought to himself, *I should test my people to see if they are really what they seem.* He then transformed into a beautiful golden eagle. He flew over the sky, watching over his people. He saw they were killing his precious animals, like the lion and the rhino.

When Joko was ready to burst out in anger, a small man saw him.

He shouted, 'A golden eagle, what a feast that would make!'

So he gathered together a group of strong men with bows and arrows. They shot their arrows and several of them hit Joko in the stomach.

When Joko fell to the ground, they surrounded him. Joko transformed into his normal self right in front of them and they were shocked that what they had shot down was their god.

Joko exclaimed that every person that had shot an arrow in any animal would die and become a star. Thousands of men and women died, so the people that were left wept all day for two weeks.

Joko felt sorry for his people, so he made more men and women who looked like their loved ones and now there was peace. Joko made a final announcement: 'If any man or woman kills a golden eagle, they shall become a star.'

And with a flash of light, Joko became the biggest and brightest star in the sky.

Samuel Knott (12)
St Bede's RC High School, Blackburn

The Stars

A long, long time ago, when the world was new, there was a great god named Zodiac. Zodiac controlled everything! The heavens bowed down and worshipped him and once he had an idea, there was no one who could change his mind. He ruled the planets and the Earth, the animals and the plants, the oceans and the fish, and most important of all, the day and the night.

Every morning Zodiac would light up a ball of fire and roll it across the sky throughout the day. As the sun got to the end of the sky, Zodiac would pull on his gigantic golden cords and a thick black curtain would be drawn across the sky, blocking out all of Earth's natural light and leaving it in complete darkness. As dawn broke up in the heavens, Zodiac would open his curtains and begin rolling the ball. This ball is better known as the sun.

Sometimes, when the servants of Earth had behaved well and shown gratitude towards the gods, he would take an opal from his palace wall and hang it in front of the curtain, giving a little light in order for the inhabitants of Earth to see. This opal was given the name moon and changed shape over a period of time.

One hot and dusty day down on Earth, when the sun shone high in the light blue sky, three of the most respected animals got together and held a meeting. The three representatives were the mosquito, the antelope and the cheetah. They had come together to discuss the matter of the night, and each one of them had the same complaint. They needed more light in the sky at night.

'Why don't we ask Zodiac the almighty if he could possibly get rid of night and for it to be never-ending day?' suggested the antelope.

'No!' roared the cheetah. 'How on earth would we sleep? The sun is far too bright and would keep us awake. I need my rest!'

'I have only one suggestion,' buzzed the mosquito. 'To simply ask Zodiac what it is that he would be prepared to do in order to give the Earth more light at night.'

All the animals ignored the little mosquito and carried on quarrelling about the problem which caused so much trouble. But in the end they agreed with the mosquito and set off to ask Zodiac about the solutions they had come up with.

Zodiac was up in the heavens, surrounded by maids who fed him red grapes and handed him goblets of fine, rich wines. So, as you can imagine, he was not best pleased when he saw the three creatures climbing the spiral staircase leading to paradise.

'Ha, more light! Don't make me laugh! You ungrateful little so and sos have everything you have because of me, and yet you ask for more! I think you had better leave before I banish you from the whole of infinity *forever!*'

So the creatures miserably set off back home. As the sun began to set, the rhino turned to the cheetah and said, 'We should have known not to take advice from the likes of him.' And with saying this he looked down at the mosquito who had hidden away in a sycamore tree, afraid to show his face.

Night-time came and the curtain was drawn. Feeling so angry and annoyed, the little mosquito flew straight at the curtain, not stopping and picking up speed. At this rate he was going to smash straight into the evil fabric, and *whoosh!* A gleaming streak of silvery light beamed through the enlarged curtain. But that wasn't all. Before the little mosquito knew what had happened, all the other insects for miles around came charging at the curtain. Holes of all shapes and sizes appeared.

At the end of this scenario, the curtain was full of speckles of light. Tiny holes that had been made by the dragonfly, smaller holes that had been made by the butterflies and even smaller holes that had been made by the mosquitoes.

These flickers of light that appeared in the night sky came to be known as the stars and were loved by everyone throughout the universe!

Jade Taylor (12)
St Bede's RC High School, Blackburn

The Coyote And The Tiger

A long time ago, in the heart of the Canadian forest, there was a small coyote who sat lonely, every night, in a hole concealed with vegetation.

But one night, when the coyote was sleeping, he was woken by an uncomfortable rumbling noise. The coyote thought it was another animal in the forest, but when this started getting frequent, the coyote got very annoyed. So that night the coyote crawled lazily out of his hole to go and have a look at what it was. As soon as the coyote lifted its head, it noticed small, bright sparkles. The coyote then thought he should try and get a closer view. He walked past many trees and lakes until he reached a wide area covered with lots and lots of minute rocks. There, sat staring, was a great variety of animals.

When the group began talking, many ideas were shared.

A snake suggested, 'They're small flies in the sky.'

A turtle suggested, 'They're all just hallucinating.'

But when the coyote suggested the moon had shattered into millions of pieces, everyone paused for a second or two and all of a sudden broke out with deafening laughter. The coyote's cheeks turned as red as cherries. He then rushed off, even too embarrassed to speak.

When everything was quiet and he wasn't embarrassed, he heard small footsteps plodding along behind him. The coyote turned around and saw a tiger, who said to him, 'I think your suggestion was great, because it's true, we don't have any moonlight anymore, just light from the tiny sparkles.'

As the tiger rushed off, the coyote got a cheeky grin.

Soon after, the coyote was home and snuggled up in his bed, but sneakily, the tiger told everyone who had laughed at him the truth and as the night wore on, more and more animals believed him. Eventually, everyone who believed him went off in a group to find the coyote.

That very night all who believed him sat down, thinking of what to call the small sparkles. Finally they came to the decision that they would be called 'stars'.

After that day, the coyote and the tiger were never to be forgotten, ever again.

Matthew Hartley (12)
St Bede's RC High School, Blackburn

The Destruction Of Earth

In the year of the mortals, when dragons ruled the skies and humans dominated the ground, Myron was an extremely intelligent, but terrible, ruler.

He had recently invented the Prozaton Laser and his plan was to take revenge on the president and the kingdom. He wanted to destroy the twelve main empires of the Earth and to harness the power of the three rings. The rings of hope, trust and harmony. With these three rings, the mad, mortifying Myron would control the Earth!

Suddenly, a hero called Neb appeared; a strapping young man with blond hair and piercing blue eyes which sparkled like the sea on a summer's day. He wore gleaming armour across his great chest. He was the general of the city, called the Bearers of the Rings. Neb and his heroic team burst through the mouth of the gates of the city on galloping, black steeds which rumbled the ground.

Neb planned to deactivate the machine before it activated. He had to destroy the Prozaton Laser before the city was under rubble. The team needed to protect the three rings!

Neb scrambled up Mount Clayton. He reached the top and found his weapon. He pressed the button, which was the wrong one. A jet of red light flew out of his weapon and he streamed backwards, falling, falling into thin air! One of Neb's team caught him and flew him back to the top. Neb called back, 'Thanks Eagle Feathers for saving my life, again!'

He ran inside and deactivated the weapon. He pulled out his gleaming, shiny weapon, then turned to face Myron. Myron slashed vigorously at his armour. Neb obliterated Myron and all that was left were a few fragments, a finger and his badge. Or was it?

Benjamin Yates (11)
St Bede's RC High School, Blackburn

The Stars Of The People

After Inti created the world, he looked at his work. The people of Peru needed light, he thought, so he appointed himself as the sun. But even gods need to sleep, so he appointed his wife, Mama-Kilya, as the moon. It is said that when she cried, she cried drops of silver. The people of Peru were happy. They grew crops and lived on them and held ceremonies to the gods. Inti was happy.

But then the people got lazy. They didn't want to spend all their time growing crops. Inti had taught them how to do it and helped them by sending rain. All they wanted to do was to kill Inti's animals and eat them. The people of Peru only held ceremonies to dance, not to worship the gods.

Inti grew angry. All the animals on Earth had a purpose and were not to be killed. So he told the people that for every animal they killed, they would have to kill a person. Sacrifice, he called it.

So people stopped killing animals and killed their own kind, waiting for the gods to say 'enough'. They killed thousands of people - huge numbers at festivals. People danced and worshipped the gods, but they were not happy.

Mama-Kilya told Inti to tell them to stop sacrificing. Inti sent a thunderstorm as a sign to stop. People did, but were still sad, for they had lost loved ones. Inti realised they needed the meat of animals to stay healthy and was sorry for what he had done. So he told his people that they could eat every animal they could catch, except for the sacred hawk. People were joyful and the hawk was hard to catch anyway.

Mama-Kilya then told the people that every person who had died would become a star, so they could see their loved ones at night. But she warned that if they killed a hawk, a star would go missing.

People cried in happiness and began their festivals to the gods.

Jessica Burns (12)
St Bede's RC High School, Blackburn

A Speckle Of Light

Long, long ago, three planets - the sun, the moon and planet Zenia, all wanted to rule the universe. After arguing continually for days and nights, they decided to go into battle. The sun shot mighty flames at the other two planets and the moon quickly retaliated by firing great rocks back.

'I will rule the universe!' boomed across the sky from all three planets.

All through the days and nights, the skies shook as they battled and battled. Zenia was the weakest, but most definitely the quickest planet. She darted around the other two planets, dodging their missiles, desperately trying to fight back, until one day a gigantic rock from the moon hurtled towards her, blasting her into millions of small pieces. The moon and the sun were so shocked at the sight of Zenia floating around in bits that they stopped fighting and made a peace pledge to take it in turns to rule the universe.

The sun would rule one side during the day and the moon would rule the other at night, then they would swap places.

The gods now light up Zenia's millions of pieces at night, so that it reminds them of the peace pledge they made, thousands of years ago.

That is how the stars in the sky were formed.

Faye Buckley (12)
St Bede's RC High School, Blackburn

The Origin Of Day And Night

A long time ago when the Earth was new, there was east land and west land. The Earth did not rotate though, so east land was constantly in darkness, whilst west land was constantly in daylight. Neither east land nor west land knew that one continent stayed dark and the other light.

But one day, one person from east land sailed in his newly-built boat to west land. He was amazed at what he saw - daylight. It was blinding at first, but his eyes soon adjusted to it. He then saw land, it was west land. He then sailed to the coast of west land where he found a village.

He went to the village and there he was greeted by a crowd of people. They had never seen him before, so they asked where he had come from. He told the villagers about east land and by the time he had finished, they wanted to go there themselves. They could only imagine what east land was like though. When the villagers asked if they could go back to east land with him, he said that his boat was only big enough for one. When he told them that, they chased him down to the beach, where he pushed his boat out into the sea and rowed away from the west land as fast as he could.

Word of the west land spread quickly on east land and word of east land spread quickly on west land. East land wanted to see the light and west land wanted to see the darkness. Both lands knew how to build boats, but they couldn't keep sailing back and forth between east land and west land, so both lands were stuck for what to do.

So they started to complain. The all-seeing and ever-seeing almighty god, Jolt, heard about this. He was stuck for what to do. But then he had an ingenious idea. He was going to rotate the Earth continuously.

When this started to happen, everybody was amazed at what they saw. But after a few years everybody, both on east land and west land, got used to it and eventually it was named day and night.

Alex Curran (11)
St Bede's RC High School, Blackburn

How The Stars Came To Be

Long, long ago in the Jurassic period lived the creator of the moon, Earth, creatures and sky. Cosmo was his name. Cosmo did great things, but to do these great things he had to do terrible things. Cosmo had noticed that at night, only the moon gave out light, so he told all the dinosaurs to meet him at Lake Mien. So one by one came all the dinosaurs and they had a meeting about what should be done about this darkness.

'We should put water in the sky to make it look lighter,' T-rex suggested.

'No, water will fall out of the sky like rain,' Cosmo answered.

'We should put more moons in the sky,' Stegosaurus shouted.

'No, the sky will collapse on us,' said Cosmo.

'Let's put silver dots in the sky. They won't fall down as rain and they're not too heavy, so the sky won't collapse on us,' Brachypodosaurus smartly said.

'Yes, but what do we use to make them silver?' Cosmo questioned.

Nobody knew, but in Cosmo's dream he had an idea. He would change all of the dinosaurs' blood to silver and then he would kill them and for every drop of blood shed, a shiny star would float about the night sky to make it lighter.

So this is what he did. But the gods were not too pleased, so they killed Cosmo and put him on the moon. So when you say there is a man on the moon, you're really seeing Cosmo.

Rhys Dea (12)
St Bede's RC High School, Blackburn

The Creation Of The Stars

A long, long time ago, before the creation of the Earth and the universe, the gods were sat in their palace debating about their perfect universe.

'Let's make it green,' said the god of plants.

'No, it has to have living beings in it. How about worlds for them to live on?' said another.

'Calm down,' shouted Zeus. 'We will use lots of different things like green plants and worlds, but we need something to explain how the universe will work.'

'How about pictures of us?' said the youngest god.

'How about flaming balls, so that whenever we get mad we can fire one at a planet,' said the god of anger.

The gods argued and argued until the early hours of the morning. Finally, they came up with a solution. The answer to their problem was stars. The stars were flaming balls scattered around the universe. Finally the gods were happy and could rest.

Now when we look into the sky at night, we see the stars and we know that the gods are looking down on us.

Anthony Farrell (12)
St Bede's RC High School, Blackburn

God's New Creation

Centuries ago, God was watching over His two friends, the deer and the hare. They were arguing over things they didn't have.

'I want more light, it is so useless up here in the mountains,' shouted the deer.

'The sun and the moon are our light. We don't need any more. But everything is so dull and boring. We need more beautiful things in our lives,' said the hare.

God was not happy. He decided to teach them a lesson. For one day He would make a total eclipse. Light would be taken away. They wouldn't be able to see any of the lovely objects he had created.

Next day, the hare and the deer started to walk up the mountain to have a siesta. As if they had been blindfolded, their vision was totally blank. They panicked and prayed for the light to reappear, promising never to complain again.

Suddenly, the moon came back into view once again. The hare and the deer had definitely learnt their lesson. God decided to make a new creation which would look so wonderful and give out light and that everyone would notice. So He made the stars and they still shine for us today!

Rebecca Fishwick (11)
St Bede's RC High School, Blackburn

How The Stars Came Into Being

A long time ago, when the Earth was ruled by the most powerful god ever known, there lived a man, a man called David. He wasn't bad enough to go to Hell, but he wasn't good enough to go to Heaven.

David died 45,000,000 years ago. This was when he was the first man that Heaven could not take. God did not know what to do with him. He decided to make a place where people like David should go. He would name it the sky.

God thought the sky must be orange, so David would stand out. He clicked his fingers and far above him was orange, bright orange.

God grabbed the jar containing David's soul to take to the sky, but while this was going on the Devil heard about it. He was so mad that David's soul was not coming to Hell, that he made the sky black, pitch-black. When God arrived outside and saw a great mass of darkness above his head, he was shocked. He was angry. God had only thought of putting David's soul just under the sky. But God was so mad his eyes turned yellow. He threw David's soul in the sky.

David's soul is now a ball of yellow in the sky. Souls which are like David's end up joining his. They did not take the warning that bad souls will not be sent to Heaven. They will be bright yellow. They will stand out. Everyone will know what will happen if they turn bad like David.

More and more souls (stars) join David's every day. They did not take the warning.

Dominique Flood (12)
St Bede's RC High School, Blackburn

How The Stars Were Made

One night on the planet of Zygo, two aliens were lying down. These were no ordinary aliens, they were as clever as anyone could ever be.

One said to the other, 'I'm bored, what should we do?'

The other intelligent alien replied, 'Why don't we make a whole new universe, but some kind of miniature one?'

So the two aliens set off to the making machine. All night and all day, these aliens programmed for a miniature universe to be made. Then, after three days of waiting, a jar rapidly popped out.

Suddenly, one of the aliens cried out, 'It's here! It's here!'

The jar was bursting with balls of gas and planets floating around inside it.

Suddenly, one said to the other, 'Don't you think it's a bit dark?'

The other alien replied, 'What should we do?' Then he had an idea. 'Why don't we put diamonds around the outside of the jar?'

But they had one problem. They had nothing to stick the diamonds onto the jar with.

The brainiest alien in 0.01 seconds gasped and said, 'I've got it! Why don't we stick the diamonds on with Superglue?'

That's how the stars were made.

Peter Hinnigan (12)
St Bede's RC High School, Blackburn

How Stars Were Made

For many years the world had been divided into two parts. There was the light part and the dark part. The light part was ruled by a god named Ra and the dark part was ruled by a god named Hades. The reason for this was because both of the gods wanted to rule the world by themselves, and because of this the people of the divided world grew more miserable and depressed every day.

But what would the solution be? Eventually, the gods realised just what they had been doing and they had to act quickly, because if they did not, the people of the world would not love them anymore. Who would be the ruler of the world? Should it be Hades, or even Ra? Then the problem was solved, and both gods ruled the world with the colossal amount of power. The world was now perfect and both gods had a crucial role to play. For Ra, the role he had to play was to look after the period of time that was light; he named it day. Hades was just as important too. He had to look after the period of time that was dark; he named it night.

But still, even after that problem was solved, another arose. This problem was even more detrimental than the previous one. This new problem was that the temperature during the day was boiling hot and the nights were far too dark - so dark that the people of the world could not see.

What would be the solution this time? Now, both gods tried to work out what the answer would be to solve the problem. Then Ra realized what it should be. The sun. So Hades stumbled over to the sun and totally smashed the outer layer of it.

The fragments flew to every region within the universe. And that was the problem solved. Something that seemed impossible was now true. The days were now perfect. So were the nights. And each fragment that was from the sun's outer layer lit up the pitch-black nights. Hades called them stars.

And ever since that time when Hades and Ra ruled, the world has never faced a greater dilemma.

Nathan Kennedy (12)
St Bede's RC High School, Blackburn

My Myth Of How The Stars Came To Be

Once there were two very powerful gods called Hyas and Pleiades, who both ruled the Earth and sky. Hyas ruled the light half called day and Pleiades ruled the dark half called night. They told the people on Earth that they should bow down and worship them only.

One day, as Hyas was sitting watching the people work, he noticed that two of the people were sitting talking and not working. Hyas wanted to know what they were saying, so he sent down some sort of insect to listen. The insect had gone down that day and heard what they had been discussing. The insect came back up to the sky and told Hyas that the people said they were tired of always worshipping the gods and wanted a break. When Hyas and Pleiades heard this, they were raging with anger, so they decided that they would take away their water and food to teach them a lesson.

So the next day, Hyas and Pleiades killed all the animals, plants and crops and made the sun hotter than any other time, to evaporate the water.

It had been days since the gods had taken away the food from the people. Most of them were ill and some had died of hunger.

The following day all the people were dead. When it became night, Pleiades realised that taking away the people's food had killed them, so both gods decided to put them in the sky at night and call them stars. This would remind the gods never to take away their people's food and water again.

Katrina Kenny (12)
St Bede's RC High School, Blackburn

The Legend Of Beowulf

Through the dark night, the silhouette shimmered. The baleful ornament strolled down from the moors, over high, high bolsters, mawkish growths, over more hills, over rippling rivers. It stumbled towards the hall, vast and furry and almost slouching. It swerved to and fro.

All the Geats guarding Heorot had fallen asleep; one man snoring, one man muffling and one man choking. Only one man was awake. He was watching.

For a few moments it waited outside the hall. Its hair bristled, its heart pounded. Then it grasped the handle and burst open the door. It ploughed forward out of the darkness into the candlelight. It took a great big step across the slippery floor and under its breath it muttered, 'Grendel!' That was the name of the monster; the symbol of darkness and greed.

Grendel, glaring at the heaped warriors, grabbed hold of the closest gentleman, scooped him up with one claw and choked the scream in his throat. The monster dug his fangs into his tender flesh and ripped him apart like paper in a shredder. The hot blood spurted out and showered Grendel from head to toe. He devoured huge pieces and within one minute he was yesterday's news. This made Grendel more covetous.

The stench was portentous. Grendel slobbered spittle and blood. He reached out for Beowulf, but Beowulf leapt up and stayed the monster's outstretched arms. Beowulf wouldn't let go. Grendel tugged and tugged. The room boomed. Clangs and clatters shattered the night silence as they dodged to and fro in their tug of war.

The Geats clashed Grendel with their swords. The warriors did not know that not even the finest iron on Earth could wound their opponent. His skin was as tough as old rind. He'd cursed himself against every kind of battle blade.

Beowulf grabbed Grendel's arm and slowly twisted, putting terrible pressure on his shoulder. Grendel surrendered. His whole body jerked and shuddered. With abnormal strength, he tried to escape Beowulf's grip. He jerked again and all at once. Grendel's right shoulder ripped! Grendel howled. He staggered away from the hall and Beowulf.

The Geats cheered and shouted. Gasping, Beowulf announced, I avenged Leofric.'

Robyn Taylor (12)
St Bede's RC High School, Blackburn

The Legend Of Beowulf

The figure floated the moors. Through the heather a sinister monster glided into the dark country.

The river was gurgling in the background where the creature was waiting on the doorstep of the Geats' meeting place. They were there sleeping like babies.

Leofric was on guard. He scrambled to and fro past the door, but with tiredness overtaking him, he dropped to the floor.

Beowulf, another Geat, knew something was wrong and he knew who to suspect. 'Grendel,' Beowulf whispered.

Outside, the creature, Grendel, waited to pounce on the sleeping Geats. A minute passed. In a flash the monster raced into the dark, dim and dismal hall. But all the Geats lay sleeping as if nothing had happened. Beowulf leapt to his feet, jumped onto the back of Grendel and started to wrestle with him.

Leofric tried to help him with his silver-bladed sword, but before he could reach him, the monster scooped him up like an ice cream and ate him whole. Hot blood spilled out of his mouth. Beowulf, Leofric's friend, became stronger.

The howl from Grendel woke up the other Geats. They made deep slices in the rough, leather skin, but the skin began to heal.

Beowulf was like a super hero. He pulled and pulled at Grendel. Grendel feared for the first time in his life. Beowulf pulled his arm off and the blood poured out. The creature hobbled away. They all cheered and lifted the arm up. Beowulf was also lifted up in the air in celebration.

Natalie Peary (11)
St Bede's RC High School, Blackburn

The Legend Of Beowulf

Across the windswept, misty moor shrithed an unknown being. A few miles away was a castle - an overpowering stone castle, with many spires and towers. The castle had no idea what was about to strike. The guards were fast asleep after guarding the castle all day. While the Geats were celebrating, the unknown abomination struck the castle door with one mighty claw.

The door swung off its hinges and the vile thing staggered through the archway. Everyone screamed, except one man. He muttered, 'Grendel!' through his clenched teeth. This man was known as Beowulf. Not much scared this six-foot high, muscular man. As he watched, Grendel lunged for a sleeping guard, Leofric. He attacked, tore, mauled and devoured him.

After the massacre, he did the same to everyone in the palace. After this, muscle, flesh, veins and blood dripped from his mouth. With all his strength and an outstretched arm, he lunged at Beowulf. Beowulf grabbed Grendel's arm and twisted it behind his neck. Putting excessive pressure on Grendel's arm, Beowulf pulled the arm towards himself.

Grendel knew he had met a power greater than his own. He bellowed. This awoke the guards and they charged towards him. Grendel was protected by a spell, meaning he was invincible to blades. Grendel's arm was severed and pulled off. He bellowed, while the blood was pouring out. Grendel fled out of the castle, while Beowulf hung the arm on a wooden beam, with blood dripping to the floor. He had defeated Grendel.

Ruari McGlone (11)
St Bede's RC High School, Blackburn

Beowulf

Crunch. Crunch. A ghostly figure lurched through the green, dense forest. The bulk was like a shadow slithering through a sewage tunnel. At last, the whole of Heorot was in the palm of his hand. The mahogany doors could not keep him out as the large, hairy, stinky beast charged in.

One person heard the doors open. He squinted his eyes. He remembered who it was because he had encountered him before in the Longstead forest. He muttered under his breath the most forbidden word in Heorot - 'Grendel.'

Grendel surged his way forward through the batch of guards. He noticed a plump Geat and instinctively his mind thought, *juicy!* He then sank his claws into the Geat's lungs before he could scream. Grendel shredded the Geat to pieces, but the Geats still slept in the bloody Heorot.

The ferocious beast turned to a meaty man. He froze on the spot. He knew this Geat. Could it be? Could it be Grendel's worst enemy, Beowulf? He had always wanted to devour Beowulf with his rotten teeth. He lunged at him. He was stopped by the hand of Beowulf and Grendel's stone heart began to beat more than it ever had before.

Beowulf threw Grendel across the hall. Grendel went for Beowulf's neck, but his hand was gripped and was wrenched behind his back. The pressure built up and up. Grendel then tugged and blood, meat, gristle and bone stained Heorot's walls. He swore he'd kill Grendel. Grendel hobbled away with his arm in his hand.

Daniel Eccles (12)
St Bede's RC High School, Blackburn

The Legend Of Beowulf

Through the darkness of the night, only the owls and the monsters lived. The creature travelled over the steepest mountains, through the muddy rivers, over the wobbly bridges and through the forest to reach Heorot.

At Heorot, all there was to see was Geats asleep. One was snoring, one coughing and one sneezing. All asleep except one, Beowulf. The Geat sneezing in the corner was called Leofric.

The creature who had travelled high and low was now stood in the forest waiting for his dinner. The creature was saying to himself, *'Grendel's going to get you!'* Grendel crept up to Leofric, but into his neck and ate him up, leaving only blood on the floor. Beowulf watched Grendel sneak into Heorot.

In Heorot, only candlelights shone and plain old paintings hung on the wall. Grendel strolled down the hall, searching for something to eat. Beowulf followed Grendel up and down. Grendel stopped and started sniffing. Beowulf jumped out and gripped Grendel with his arm pushed against his back. Grendel was trying to escape, but Beowulf's pressure was too strong. Growling and whining noises came from Grendel's mouth. Beowulf pulled Grendel's arm. You could hear the bones crack and the muscle rip. All the other Geats came running in with their weapons.

Grendel ran away with only one arm. All the Geats celebrated, hugging each other and cheering.

'I don't think we will see him again,' said Beowulf.

Hayley Stanley (12)
St Bede's RC High School, Blackburn

The Legend Of Beowulf

Over the marsh a shady figure crept. Across the gurgling stream, leaping over the hills and twisting around paths.

At Heorot all the Geats were asleep. All except one - Beowulf. One Geat was snoring, one grunting and one shuffling in his bed. All not knowing what was going to happen next.

The shadowy figure burst open the doors of Heorot and breathed deeply in delight. Shambling across the room went the thing.

Beowulf saw him and under his breath grunted, 'Grendel.'

Meanwhile, Grendel was staring with an unearthly grin on his face at a stocky, brave warrior called Leofric. Grendel grabbed the man and gouged the yell out of his mouth. With one fatal swipe, Grendel threw Leofric across the room, then ripped his body to finish him off. One by one, piece by piece, Grendel devoured Leofric in seconds.

Beowulf pulled a face in disgust. He jumped out of his bed and ran towards Grendel. Beowulf got Grendel into a tight headlock and Grendel screamed in fright. Each one pulled a different way until Beowulf's hand slipped down Grendel's arm. Beowulf had an idea. He twisted Grendel's arm upwards and he ripped it off. Hot, thick blood spurted everywhere. The scream of the beast woke up all the other Geats. One by one the brave Geats picked up their swords and started to slash the beast fearlessly. But this would not work. Grendel had concocted a potion that made man-made weapons ineffective against him.

Grendel pulled away and ran out.

'You did well. No living being can live with that sort of wound,' said the oldest and wisest Geat.

'I wanted to kill him,' breathed Beowulf.

Grendel never bothered Heorot again. In fact, he died the very next day.

Elizabeth Mercer (12)
St Bede's RC High School, Blackburn

The Legend Of Beowulf

The creature shrithed down from the moors over gurgling streams and over sheep runs, and down to the Geats' stronghold - Heorot. He grasped the iron gates and tore his way into Heorot. He leapt into the candlelight and pounced on the nearest warrior, then growled with hunger.

Leofric, a brave Geat, was sitting down when he was struck with the mighty creature's strength.

Another warrior named Beowulf, through gritted teeth whispered one word - 'Grendel.'

Meanwhile, Grendel was devouring Leofric with tremendous power. He ripped through Leofric's skin and drank the blood from his veins, then swallowed him bit by bit.

Suddenly, Beowulf jumped on Grendel, drove him back and gave him one mighty blow. For once in his life, Grendel felt fear. Beowulf held Grendel on the floor, grappling him and keeping Grendel's arms stationary. Grendel's only goal was to escape. Beowulf twisted the hideous creature's arm around his back slower and slower. Muscles cracked and Grendel howled with pain as his arm eased off. Hot blood spurted out. Grendel staggered out of Heorot with only one arm.

The king of Heorot proclaimed, 'Beowulf shall be the next king when I die!'

Joshua Burke (12)
St Bede's RC High School, Blackburn

The Legend Of Beowulf

A strange shadow crept through the dark night. Its feet pounded. All of a sudden it fell and made a huge bang.

Beowulf heard this racket from the king's castle. He knew who it was. It had wanted to eat the king for as long as he could remember. Beowulf had guarded the king for 20 years. He couldn't give up now. 'It's Grendel!' he yelled. 'Wake up!' But his friends were all asleep. He was the littlest of the Geats. He didn't want to take on that monstrous bulk alone.

Big footsteps boomed closer. He wanted to run, but the freakish creature was now towering over him. Beowulf froze with fright. Grendel grabbed three sleeping Geats. He devoured them as appetisers.

Grendel seemed ready for his main meal - the king. He spun round and aimed at Beowulf. Beowulf ducked out of the way and stuck his sword into Grendel's leg. Grendel laughed with pity and pulled the blood-covered sword out. He flicked it over the castle wall and chuckled. Blood started to pour from the wound. He bent over and started to lick his bloody leg.

Beowulf grabbed Grendel's other arm and twisted it. It cracked. Grendel roared. He pulled away and flesh and muscle started to tear. Blood started to pour. Suddenly, click, crack, crunch - his arm dropped to the ground. Grendel gave one last roar and collapsed.

The Geats chanted, 'Grendel is dead!'

The king knighted Beowulf. He became army general and the Geats' hero!

Stevie Walmsley (12)
St Bede's RC High School, Blackburn

Beowulf

Across the fields lived the most frightening monster imaginable. Its teeth were as black as charcoal and its fur was as brown as bark. Its eyes were as green as its own slime and its heart was smaller than a bean.

The beast's target was the great timbered hall of Heorot, but to get there it had to pass through the guards. They were all asleep except for one - Leofric. The beast came and killed Leofric. It ate his body in chunks from his eyeballs to his toes. It ate every scrap, it even drank his blood.

Beowulf, friend of Leofric, heard about this and he was disgusted. Beowulf confronted the beast and under his breath he muttered one word - 'Grendel.'

For the first time in his life, Grendel felt fear. He knew Beowulf would not spare his life if he got his hands on him.

The fight lasted only a few minutes. Beowulf bent Grendel's arm back so far, he heard a crack. Grendel was in incredible pain and then, with one more tug, his arm tore off. Beowulf knew the beast didn't have long to live.

Later that night, crowds gathered to welcome Beowulf. The cheers were amazing. One of Beowulf's past enemies came up to him and begged for his forgiveness.

So from that day forward, he was respected by everyone. He had done Leofric proud.

Oliver Houldsworth (11)
St Bede's RC High School, Blackburn

The Legend Of Beowulf

It, shambled along the moors, past the gurgling stream and up to the Geats' castle, in Heorot. It approached the metal railing and prised open the bars, then walked up to the huge black door, clenched the ring handle and pulled it open. It walked in. It then jumped onto the nearest Geat and ate him whole.

There was one man watching - Beowulf. It, had just killed one of his friends. Beowulf was really angry. Beowulf wanted revenge.

It, crept through the hall doors. Through a small gap in Beowulf's teeth, he whispered, 'Grendel.'

Beowulf slowly moved out of his seat. Then he slammed his drink onto the table. Grendel spun round. Beowulf stepped up to Grendel and whispered to himself, *war!*

Beowulf leapt onto Grendel's arm, clenched it with all his might, twisted it round his back and jerked it. Grendel howled with pain! Beowulf still kept jerking Grendel's arm. Then, all of a sudden, Grendel's arm dislocated and was detached away from his shoulder. He shrieked and rattled the whole building.

Beowulf then stepped away from Grendel and left him to bleed to death.

Everyone cheered, for Beowulf was a hero. The Geats partied for many days after than and Beowulf remains a hero today.

Nicholas Hoyle (12)
St Bede's RC High School, Blackburn

Beowulf

Through the dark, misty night, a terrifying inauspicious figure snuck through the town, looking everywhere as it came. Unexpectedly, in the distance, it heard a strange buzzing noise. As it inched closer, the noise became louder. It moved closer then stopped to listen. It moved. Then stopped. Then moved. Then stopped. It listened carefully to the noise, then knew at once. It was Geats, his favourite meal.

As it licked its lips, it hurtled towards them. Suddenly, there was a loud screeching noise as one of the Geats, Leofric, was snatched from sleeping, ripped open and devoured bit by bit. Slowly it sucked out his blood and slurped it down with a generous helping of flesh.

Rapidly, a dark, vicious figure named Beowulf, woke and grabbed the monster. 'Grendel,' he muttered.

He picked him up and tugged at his arm. Grendel yelled out a roar of pain as his arm ripped out of its socket and landed on a pile of crunching leaves on the floor. Grendel fell to the ground with blood squirting out, like someone was squeezing a bottle of ketchup. Then all the other Geats woke up and cheered.

The Geats then prepared a big celebration which lasted all through the night. From that day on, Beowulf became a hero.

Abigail McCann (11)
St Bede's RC High School, Blackburn

The Legend Of Beowulf

There it was, pounding over the hill. An immense figure shaking the ground as it came. With big, hairy hands and long, slim legs, it came closer to a bony, young man. He lay awake guarding the giant gates of Heorot.

The young man watched the shape get closer and shouted, *'It's Grendel!'* he didn't move though, he didn't even twitch.

Grendel was just one metre away. Saliva dripped from his steaming mouth as he towered over the tiny man. The man began to shiver and tried to escape. But instead of being scared and running away, he faced everyone's fear - Grendel.

The man muttered, 'I, Beowulf, will defeat you.'

Then a sudden fight broke out. With clanging and banging, crashing and lashing, the battle commenced. Blood flew across the yard and punches were flung. Grendel had fear flooding his grizzly face. Beowulf took one last blow and grabbed Grendel's beastly arm behind his head and he tugged and heaved. Grendel gave out horrific squeals as Beowulf carried on heaving.

After what seemed like hours, Grendel's arm was in Beowulf's hand. He had done it! Grendel staggered away with no hope to live. His one arm hung loosely by his immense feet.

Beowulf had to go and tell everyone, so he jumped for joy and ran to the others in the yard. He was so excited. He had defeated everyone's worst enemy. 'I am a champion!' he called as he skipped in Grendel's dusty footprints.

Michaela Gallacher (12)
St Bede's RC High School, Blackburn

The Legend Of Beowulf

On the dark moor, a figure crept up to Heorot. Its heart was beating and throbbing. It pounced through the window, grabbing and instantly killing the nearest guard. The monster had just introduced himself to Heorot. Its name was Grendel.

Grendel was amazed that after all that noise, not one guard had stirred. He would make them pay for their insolence, so he turned upon his nearest victim.

He was wrong, as one guard *had* stirred and was up. His name was Beowulf. Beowulf crept behind Grendel and grabbed his left arm. He then put Grendel in an unbreakable lock.

As his friends awoke, Beowulf knew that if he let go, every guard in Heorot house would be massacred, just like the other guard.

Grendel knew that if he didn't get out of the guard's grasp, he would die, as the guard was dismantling him piece by piece. Grendel pulled and pulled and let out an ear-piercing scream that went right through Beowulf. Grendel's arm came off, the blood was seeping onto the floor and Grendel sprinted off howling.

In the hall of Heorot, everyone was ecstatic. The guards who had survived jumped up and down as if they had just won a world war.

Grendel was trying his best to get home. He knew he would die if he didn't. Then he started spluttering and he fell, instantly dead.

Joseph Smith (12)
St Bede's RC High School, Blackburn

The Legend Of Beowulf

It was a very cold and misty autumn night and all the soldiers from the National Guard were asleep on their night duty. The door suddenly opened and a large figure stood in the doorway. One man woke straight away, but he wished he hadn't because the figure smelt of death and the smell was choking him. Under his breath he kept repeating, *Grendel!*

Grendel heard Beowulf and he suddenly spun around. He didn't see who spoke, but Beowulf was shivering. Grendel was bloodthirsty, so he roared that loud that the whole building shook. Then he grabbed the first man he saw and choked the scream out of him, then consumed Leofric in one gulp.

Beowulf leapt off his chair to seek his revenge on Grendel because he had killed Leofric, and he couldn't bear the sight or smell of Grendel. He grabbed Grendel by the arm and spun him around. It was very hard for Beowulf to fight Grendel, as he was tired and weak, but he tried his best.

Beowulf persistently yanked Grendel's arm, but it made no difference. Finally, Beowulf yanked Grendel's arm so hard, it came off and Grendel howled in pain. The blood coming from Grendel's arm smelt like death and it was so hot that steam came off it when it hit the floor.

Grendel slashed Beowulf, before running away into the wilderness. Beowulf was badly hurt and he still had hold of Grendel's arm. He woke everybody up once he had got to his feet and they were all happy.

Polly Hindle (12)
St Bede's RC High School, Blackburn

Beowulf

From across the dark cornfields and the slivering streams came a dark, sinister creature. Its eyes were scarlet-red and the finest hairs covered its beastly body.

The timbered hall was the target. He shambled across the farm and waited outside, ready to pounce at any moment.

Inside the hall, guards were weary, all clustered together like a knot, when suddenly a scratching noise was heard at the door.

The guards were awake now and two guards ambled towards the door. Trembling and scared, the guards stood still.

The beast, known as Grendel, slashed down the door and splinters flew at the nearest guard. Grendel charged at a soldier named Leofric and devoured him. Licking his lips, he ambled towards another guard but couldn't make it, because a brave soldier named Beowulf leapt out of his reaching grasp, tugged one of his arms and twisted it round his back.

Grendel grunted with pain and tried to break free. Soldiers grabbed their spears and tried to wound the beast. Grendel knew he was impervious to any battle blade. Beowulf eased the pain then twisted the arm the other way.

The guards stood watching Grendel grunting away. Just then a tearing noise issued from the beast's arm. A spurt of blood and pieces of muscle jumped out.

Beowulf let go and Grendel ran away into the darkness of the field.

'What shall we do with his arm?' asked the splintered guard.

'Burn it for Leofric,' Beowulf said as he gazed at the moon.

Sam McGlynn (12)
St Bede's RC High School, Blackburn

Beowulf

Grendel's skin glistened like polished bronze in the moonlight. He shrithed across the moors and marshes. His large, bulky package ruined the silence of night. He came across the great gate of Heorot, where four guards were asleep, but one was not - one brave guard of the Geats.

The young Geat whispered, like a rustle of leaves, 'Grendel.'

Grendel ate one of the guards, devouring the limbs, crunching the bones, chewing the flesh ravenously.

'Leofric!' Beowulf cried. His beloved friend had been killed.

He wanted revenge, like a hungry bear wanted fish. Beowulf had no fear of the monster, he prowled for his prey, then attacked. He gripped Grendel's arm tightly, putting immense pressure on it. Grendel felt fear for the very first time and it killed his confidence, slowly, very slowly.

Despite the increasing noise, Heorot remained in a deep sleep.

Beowulf pulled tightly on Grendel's arm. The Geats awoke and grabbed the finest weaponry. Neither pitchfork nor slingshot could kill Grendel as he had many spells cast on him, including one that prevented weapons from hurting him.

Beowulf could feel Grendel's weakness, his determination to be loose of Beowulf's grip, but it wasn't working.

Still the Geats battled for their revenge, trying with all their might to kill and destroy Grendel.

Grendel pulled hard and his arm was torn from its socket. Hot blood trickled down the toughened skin.

The Geats cheered as Grendel ran, finally free, never to be seen by the Geats again.

Katrina Leaf (12)
St Bede's RC High School, Blackburn

Beowulf

It was a dark night. An even darker figure slid through the marshes. Its fierce arm swung. It was tall and looked terrifying. It was walking closer and closer.

All the guards were asleep on the ground near the marshes, except one who was standing wide awake.

The fierce figure carried on moving closer and closer. No one could hear it and only Leofric could see it. He muttered under his breath, 'Grendel.'

When Grendel entered the old hall, he struck at Leofric, Beowulf watched out of his half-open eye. That's when the big fight began.

Grendel scooped up Beowulf's arm and started twisting it behind his back. He twisted and twisted and twisted, until you could smell hot blood pouring from Beowulf's arm. You could hear the cracking of the veins and the tearing of the muscles. Beowulf's arm dropped to the ground.

Everyone started to cheer, Grendel had defeated Beowulf and the spell had been broken.

Helen Moore (12)
St Bede's RC High School, Blackburn

The Legend Of Beowulf

Through the moors it roamed. Its sinister shadow swiftly made its way towards the hut.

In Heorot, all the Geats were asleep - all but one. Beowulf was awake.

For a moment it waited outside, then slowly it opened the door. Though he was half asleep, Beowulf whispered, 'Grendel.'

In a flash, Grendel pounced onto a Geat named Leofric. Grendel bit into him, slurped all his blood and had swallowed him whole in less than a minute.

Beowulf jumped up, grabbed hold of his sword and started stabbing and slashing at Grendel. But it was no use. Grendel had put a spell on himself which prevented him getting hurt by any weapon.

Beowulf threw down his sword to see if he could do anything with his bare hands. He grabbed hold of Grendel's arm and turned it. Slowly he turned it and twisted it behind Grendel's back.

Grendel howled, which woke all the other Geats who started to attack Grendel. Knowing he had him in a tight grip, Beowulf yanked the green, hairy menace's arm. Grendel bawled and tugged the other way. The sounds of bones cracking and muscles ripping filled the timber hut.

Grendel scrambled out of the hut with only one arm attached to his body. A Geat picked up Grendel's arm and nailed it to the wall.

All the Geats cheered, but Beowulf didn't look happy.

'I wanted to throttle him,' gasped Beowulf.

'He's dead now, it doesn't matter,' said Andegara.

'Let's raise a toast to Leofric,' cried a Geat.

'To Leofric,' chanted all the Geats.

Chelsea Pemberton (11)
St Bede's RC High School, Blackburn

The Legend Of Beowulf

It crawled along the moors, swiftly it glided, leaving a trail of slobber on its way. Up the steps it ran and breached the walls of Heorot. No noise. No scent. It could not be tracked. It was as sly as a fox. At the door, it whispered his name, but one man heard and he was a guard.

Scratching, barging, Grendel used his giant claw to tear the wooden door to pieces. He crept through the door, choosing a man to devour. Then he struck the nearest man called Leofric, a friend of Beowulf, jumping on him from behind.

Beowulf whispered, 'Grendel.' He was frozen as the green, hunchbacked monster tore Leofric apart. Devouring the flesh and squeezing his veins, he sucked up his blood; not even a drop touched the floor.

Suddenly, Beowulf jumped out, grabbed him by the hand and arm and pulled him away. Grendel stood firm for there was no escape. Beowulf was too strong. Their fingers broke and bones were cracking, tugging each other to and fro. Both were filled with anger: Beowulf for Leofric and for Grendel it was natural. Then a muscle tore and it came from Grendel. Blood was dripping everywhere. Grendel had lost his arm. Then the monster scurried away into the darkness, leaving a trail of blood.

Beowulf cheered and woke the guards. He showed them Grendel's arm and they cheered as the monster bled to death in the darkness.

Matthew Bradley (11)
St Bede's RC High School, Blackburn

The Legend Of Beowulf

From the bleak, bitter mountains of Articus trudged a green, humpbacked apparition. Saliva was dripping onto its green, hairy, muscled chest. It was commencing its evil plan to cause death and destruction to the innocent people of Heorot.

As it saw the gates of Heorot before him, it paced up and grabbed the handle with its sweaty palms. It tugged and the gateway to Heorot opened.

'Argh, it's Grendel!' squealed a Geat warrior as they were polishing swords and debating the tactics for the civil war.

The beast came galloping in at a great speed, scooping up Geats in his path and dropping them into his hole of hunger. He spat out their remains, which were coated in thick blood and saliva, when his eye captured Beowulf scurrying towards him.

Beowulf launched his attack, sword drawn. He knew it wouldn't help as Grendel had cast a spell on himself. No weapon could harm him. As Grendel lifted his trident-like claw to slash Beowulf, Beowulf rapidly grabbed it. He twisted the arm like clockwork. He tugged and tugged. *Crack!* It was released from the socket.

'*Argh!*' Grendel let out a shriek of pain. The ligament popped out, along with a mass of green, slimy goo.

A crowd of surviving warriors flocked to where the battle took place. For days after, celebrations were held and the severed arm was given as a trophy for Beowulf's bravery.

Bianca Whittaker (12)
St Bede's RC High School, Blackburn

The Legend Of Beowulf

From across the marshes it shrithed loathsomely. Its sinister figure crept closer and closer.

It stretched out an arm. It swung the door open. It stared at the ring of warriors. Which one was first?

The warrior were asleep. Some were coughing, some were sleeping and one brave warrior lay there watching between half-closed eyes. He breathed the word, 'Grendel' the name of the monster.

Grendel scooped up a warrior, a brave warrior called Leofric, and devoured him completely.

Immediately, Beowulf pounced on Grendel and slowly pulled his arm round his back. Grendel howled and grunted with pain. He put all of his energy into breaking free, but Beowulf held firm. For once in Grendel's life he felt fear and he knew he'd met a much stronger strength than his own. Beowulf turned Grendel's arm, slowly he turned it, applying incredible pressure.

In an instant, the warriors woke up after hearing the cracking. They picked up their swords and slashed at Grendel's twisted arm. But it was no use. Grendel had put a spell on his body to make his skin as thick as old rind, so no weapon could wound him.

Then Beowulf turned Grendel's right arm a little bit more and a howl came from Grendel as his arm was taken from him. He ran out of the door into the wilderness.

'The monster is defeated!' shouted one of the warriors.

'There's no way a monster could survive such heavy wounds. No way at all!' shouted another.

'Yes!' exclaimed Beowulf. 'We have avenged Leofric's death!'

Niall Boyle (12)
St Bede's RC High School, Blackburn

Beowulf

It was a dark night and an even darker shape slid, its long arms swinging with great might and its enormous eyes gleaming. It shrived over valleys, over streams and came to the place it had been searching for.

It grabbed hold of the big, bronze door knob. Like a gorilla, it swung its arms, pushed open the door and ran onto the patterned floor.

Beowulf lay in bed. He heard the bangs. As he looked around, all the others were sleeping. He murmured the terrifying word, 'Grendel!'

Grendel rushed into the room. He clumsily picked up one of the warriors, bit into him and ate the flesh, bones and blood. The other warriors still slept.

Quickly, Beowulf grabbed hold of Grendel. He dug his fingernails into his scaly head and turned. Grendel roared for mercy. Beowulf then seized hold of Grendel's arm. He pulled and pulled. Grendel bellowed. His arm ripped off, spurting hot blood everywhere.

The warriors awoke and helped bring Grendel to the ground. They picked up his arm. The hair on it still bristled. The stench was appalling and the feel was still hard and coarse. But this was only Grendel's arm, which meant Beowulf had defeated the mighty beast. Grendel was gone and definitely forgotten.

The warriors cheered and drank to their victory. The others ate for their happiness and clapped for their joy.

Beowulf stood up, raised his head and shouted, 'My friends, I give you the amazing news - Grendel has gone!'

One warrior screamed, 'It's magnificent!'

Another bellowed, 'Great!'

This story has been passed on over centuries. Some people say it has changed, but only you know if it has!

Francesca Smith (11)
St Bede's RC High School, Blackburn

Beowulf

A tall, bulky figure was waiting stealthily outside the hall. It smelt blood. The Geats inside the hall had no idea it was watching them from the weary midnight woods.

It was edging closer by the second, while the Geats were asleep in dreamland. It was slathering at the look and taste of the Geats.

Grendel was no more than one metre away from one of them. It had one last look to check that the coast was clear and then tore off the head of one of the Geats, throwing it on the floor and chewing the rest of the body until there was nothing left but bones.

Grendel still wanted more. One of the Geats just had to wake up before another ascended to Heaven. Luckily, one did and it was the bravest and wisest of the group - Beowulf.

Beowulf woke to the ghastly figure of Grendel. He knew what had happened and straight away pounced on Grendel's back like a cheetah. Grendel, grunting and growling, was trying to fling Beowulf off his back. By this time, all the Geats were awake and encouraging Beowulf. Grendel was panicking. Beowulf twisted and turned Grendel's arm. It crunched, it cracked and then, off it came! There was a puddle of green, reeking blood. Beowulf let go of him and Grendel ran back to where he had come from.

Beowulf was a hero to the Geats. That night they had a party, but they couldn't help thinking of the poor Geat who died.

Craig Parry (12)
St Bede's RC High School, Blackburn

The Legend Of Beowulf

It came from the dark moors. It had crept over the hills then stopped. Everything was silent. The only sound was the wind banging on its face.

It looked up at the Geats. All of them were sleeping, all except one, one who was guarding the gate. The dark figure looked at the guard. It looked and looked and looked. All of a sudden, it leapt onto the man. The figure sunk its teeth into the man's neck and drank all his blood, then devoured him in one, leaving only his clothes. Still the Geats slept.

Another man looked out of a window and whispered, 'Grendel.' His name was Beowulf. He determined to kill Grendel, like Grendel had killed his friend.

Grendel shoved open the gate and limped into Heorot. When he got there, Beowulf was waiting for him. As soon as Grendel opened the door, Beowulf leapt on him. Grendel tried to throw him off, but couldn't. The Geats suddenly woke up and sprinted up to the hall.

Next, Beowulf grabbed Grendel's arm and twisted it, putting lots of pressure on his shoulder. Beowulf then ripped Grendel's arm right off. Grendel squealed with pain and charged out of Heorot.

'He won't be alive for much longer,' one Geat said.

'Yeah, he's done for,' shouted another.

All the Geats and Beowulf celebrated all night and well into the next day.

Charlotte Matthewman (11)
St Bede's RC High School, Blackburn

The Stars

One clear night, Russell was walking home from a hard day's work. It was getting late and he was getting a little tired. *I'll just have a little nap,* he thought. Russell flung down his bag and rested his head upon it. He lay on his side feeling slightly funny, as if he was being watched.

Russell was getting a little uncomfortable on his side, so he flipped over onto his back. Russell looked up. He gazed up at the sky. His heart started to beat faster. The reason he felt as though he was being watched was because he was! Millions of eyes from the dead were staring down at him.

Russell panicked, screamed and ran.

Callum Boulton (12)
St Bede's RC High School, Blackburn

The Making Of The Stars

There was once a god called Mya. Mya wanted the world to be perfect, so she made tall, green trees that would grow again after being chopped down and used for fires and shelter, animals that would be 'reborn' after being killed and eaten, and finally, humans that would use the land, plants and animals wisely.

She put them on Earth one by one. Firstly, the land - mud, rocks and grass. Then animals - herbivores and omnivores. Lastly, humans, the cleverest creatures in the world.

Everyone got on well and Mya thought everything was perfect. But, she couldn't have been more wrong!

On the third day, rain came. Nobody was prepared. They had all spent the first couple of days talking and getting to know each other. Every living thing ran for shelter, up, and under trees.

The humans knew they had to cut the trees down and kill the animals, but they didn't want to. The trees knew they had to take water from the land, but they didn't want to. The animals knew they had to either kill each other or eat the trees' leaves and grass, but they didn't want to. They liked each other too much.

Eventually, most things and people died. When Mya saw, she stormed down to Earth in a strop. Mya killed everyone and everything on Earth.

After, when she returned to the clouds, she regretted everything she had done and said. So, she gave them all a white-yellow glow. She called them stars. Now, everyone that dies becomes a star.

Daisy Boulton (12)
St Bede's RC High School, Blackburn

The Curse Of Argogola

The rats arrived in Argogola in the Middle Ages, there's no good reason why. Perhaps it was the decay of the plague that drew them, or maybe it was the curse.

There was a withered widow who lived in a shack close to Argogola. She didn't mix with the villagers, other than to administer strange herbal remedies and deliver babies. It's safe to say however innocuous she was, she wasn't normal and it's no wonder she was accused of witchcraft by the ungrateful villagers.

No one believed she was guilty, but there hadn't been a burning since May and they craved the heat and the screams. Magister Roberts gave evidence at the trial, insisting she had called the Devil to Argogola and a mother said she's invoked the Devil and gave him a home in her baby!

She was led to the stake, followed by her cat. She didn't make a sound as she was strapped to the log, but as the hay was set alight, she looked up out of newly blackened eyes and let out a horrendous howl. 'You will suffer for this deed. May your descendants live in eternal darkness from this day! Suffer I say! A curse on you!'

When her screams subsided, she began to laugh manically and finally slumped into the flames.

The heavens opened and the sky turned jet-black. And so the rats came. They thrived in the hellish conditions, but the Argogolians lived in misery for evermore, cursed for a lifetime.

Nomie Clarke (14)
St Chad's Catholic High School, Runcorn

No More

He pushed me against the wall. His strong arm held my waist. His lips touched mine and I shivered with delight. My first kiss . . . his lips moved down to my neck.

They can't tease me anymore. They can't beat me or taunt me about my looks anymore. 'Bony four-eyes' who will never get a boy, has got one!

Sharp daggers ripped through my neck. I screamed and tried to push Damon away. My vision became fuzzy. A loud whistling entered my ears. I felt my life being sucked from my body. Apart from the pain rippling through my limbs, pins and needles was the only feeling. Tears trickled down my face. My eyesight darkened and I began to slip down the wall as my knees weakened. He grabbed my shoulder. I felt and heard the bones snap and crush under his hand. My throat hurt from screaming.

He stopped, lifted his head, his eyes matching the blood dripping from his mouth. His beauty was gone. In its place, a beast. He smiled and flashed his daggers - teeth. He released my crushed shoulder. I fell, but no pain. I felt him lift my head. I opened my eyes as he held my head. He cut his skin with his nail and pulled my mouth towards it. It went black.

My eyes flew open. I used my hands to feel around. A box. I rubbed my eyes and opened them a second time. I screamed, but no one would hear me. I was dead . . .

Hazel Clarke (14)
St Chad's Catholic High School, Runcorn

A Day In The Life Of A Small Child During The Blitz

3rd September 1942

It's been nearly two years since the Blitz began and I still hear the air raid sirens ringing in my ears, the *bang, bang* of the guns, the *thump, thump* of the bombs and the bells on the fire engines and ambulances. My family are quite well off and so we have a bomb shelter outside our house, which I need not say has come in very useful. When the bombing got so near and intense, we would huddle together and sometimes a cloud of dust would come through the cracks in the doorway. The ground would shake like a dog coming out of water and it would not calm down for two, three, or even four hours. The stench of burning houses and piercing screams would burst through the door unexpectedly and uninvited.

We left the shelter as the first rays of daylight broke through the wooden slats that were makeshift windows. The heat from the Surrey Docks was so strong that wood soaked with water from firemen's hoses dried out and caught fire again. There were people running frantically, not knowing which way to go. There were children crying out for gas masks. Water was pouring down in torrents. The world was turning and yet the scene unfolding around me held no time frame. To this day, I cannot let go of the images that I saw during those days.

Now there is a glow in the sky from a country rejoicing.

Steff White (14)
St Chad's Catholic High School, Runcorn

The Island Of Terlina

The sun was shining merrily over the enchanting Indian island of Terlina. There wasn't so much as one grey cloud in the aqua sky and ever since the terrible dragon, Yulah, had vanished, villages of laughter spread across the land.

Rasmine danced gracefully around her grand bedroom as she brushed her shiny black hair and sang sweetly. She was to be the proud wife of Priula the next day and her happiness shone through golden skin. Priula, who was to be the future king of Terlina, and what a fine king he would make, with his open heart and generosity.

The sun rose bright and early the next day and the birds' music gently awoke Rasmine with a smile. She leapt out of bed and began to dress for the romantic event.

Suddenly, a huge gush of wind flew through her open window. Rasmine turned to discover that the terrible Yulah had entered her palace. She screamed for help, but in her large home she had no chance. Yulah swept her up in the air then, as fast as lightning, exited the palace via the window. It flew over the island smiling slyly at the terrified villagers below.

All of a sudden a beautiful flying carpet rose alongside Yulah. It was Priula. He bravely took out his glittering warrior sword and with one great swipe, Yulah's head dropped to the ground. Priula quickly took Rasmine into his arms and landed perfectly on the ground.

The whole island cheered as the loving couple exchanged their vows.

Erin Smith (13)
St Chad's Catholic High School, Runcorn

My Brisk Walk

I left my home and strolled along the winding paths of my street. I was enjoying the sunshine and the warm air brushing past my face. I walked through the park and into the everlasting countryside. I didn't want to go back there. If I did go back it would only lead to false hope of my father ever returning. The pain of having to watch Mother suffer and my younger brother, Ellis, not acting his usual joyful self. In all honesty, I do not believe myself strong enough to return home. I am a coward and I cannot face seeing my family fall to pieces. I'm just going to keep walking, over the flower-filled meadows, through the scenic forests, over any mountain and beyond. For no matter what, that question still persists in my mind. Why us? Why Father? Why my family and me? There are many cruel disasters in this world, but is there really any need for war?

Fern Smith (13)
St Chad's Catholic High School, Runcorn

A Day In The Life Of Macbeth

Dear Diary,

Today I thought my eyes were deceiving me . . . I came across the most unusual atmosphere; a dark, gloomy, secluded heath. This didn't frighten me in the slightest as I had just returned from battle.

On my journey, Banquo accompanied me. Then a terrible field of vision struck my eyes. Three peculiar forms of women sat in a little hut saying my name. Then followed my position of Thane of Glamis, then a weird situation hit. The announcement that travelled from the beard-growing women was two names that I did not have. Thane of Cawdor and King of Scotland. When these words reached my ears, it sent an instant shock to my brain.

I was wondering where these predictions came from, so I asked, 'Say from whence you owe this strange intelligence . . .' But came no reply. Then with the blink of an eye they were gone.

I was alarmed by the comments that were spoken. On my way home, Banquo and I had a chat and we discussed if these were predictions maybe chance would put me in place of the throne.

I assumed these were predictions because just after the three weird sisters left, the King's men appeared and announced that I was now the new Thane of Cawdor. This has left me with a scrambled brain and some shocking thoughts that keep stabbing at me, inside my head.

I am going to get my rest and I will report back to my diary tomorrow.

Lauren Caldwell (14)
St Chad's Catholic High School, Runcorn

Diary Of Paris Hilton

Dear Diary,

I woke up today to find my breakfast waiting at the end of my bed, which was left there by my butler. I quickly ate it and made my way to the pool, for my morning swim to freshen me up. I quickly dried myself and pulled one of my many Ralph Lauren suits from my wardrobe. I rang Nicole and we arranged to meet in Louis Vitton to go shopping, (my favourite hobby).

I found Nicole in the jewellery section looking at the necklaces priced at $15,000, but for us money is no object!

When we got out of the shop there were crowds surrounding us, but our bodyguards managed to squeeze us past all of them. It's times like this when you realise being famous has a lot of downsides, but if we just concentrated on them, who would be famous? Just think about the good points - I can shop, shop, shop, all day long and never worry about the finances.

At 8 o'clock I met Nicole in the VIP section of our local club. We receive first class treatment here, as we are the best customers.

I arrived home at 2 o'clock to find everyone in bed. I drank a pint of water before I went to bed to keep my skin young and soft. Anyway, I have to go now. Goodnight.

Love Paris.

Catherine Martin (13)
St Chad's Catholic High School, Runcorn

A Soldier's Life

Dear Diary,

Today was my first day out there on the battlefield. It was horrible. Everyone stared at me and shouted abusive comments. I was scared, I didn't know if they would get worse or what else they might do to me. I tried to stay strong, I thought of my family but nothing could take my mind off my surroundings.

The chief came up to me, a stern expression on his hideous face. He told me I had to do a test. Suddenly he kicked me. I fell to the floor. He kicked me harder continuously. Then he stopped. I struggled to my feet in pain. He walked off with a smirk on his face.

The other soldiers huddled together talking, as a fighter jet took to the skies. I watched it spin and twirl. Suddenly it started to dive out of control. Black smoke burst out as a flame was seen. It crashed to the ground with a thud and the ground shook. The other soldiers went silent, then turned and walked away. I didn't understand. Weren't they even going to try and save him? Was it because he was black? I watched them in disgust.

I ran to the crash zone, not knowing what I might find. I got there and I couldn't believe my eyes. I stepped back in shock and ran.

Alexandra Parkinson (14)
St Chad's Catholic High School, Runcorn

My Chapter

She did it again. Flippin' snobby Olivia. I stomped into my room, ripped off my manky blazer and threw myself onto my bed.

'Hi, Louie,' Davina muttered from behind an old and forbidden 'Cosmo'.

'Hello,' I grumbled.

'What happened?'

'O-livi-*arrr* got me told off by Mademoiselle again,' I told my pillow.

'What for?' she said, glancing up from 'Celeb Fashion Disasters'.

I lifted my head to look at her. 'Nothing!'

'Well . . .' Afternoon bell rang.

'That lecture'll have to wait!' I laughed.

'Cow!' she said as we ambled towards maths. People as posh as Davina sound messed up when they swear. 'You shouldn't leave that on the floor, it'll get creased,' she said, regarding my jacket.

'Yes, wouldn't want to ruin this *charming* emerald pinstripe,' I replied, picking at a blob of chocolate on my sleeve and frowning.

'Come on, you scruff!' she chimed.

'Not a scruff,' I muttered from beneath messy curls.

We came to the top of the stairs and immediately something was wrong. There was a steady *drip, drip* of water off a table, on which stood a vase . . . except it didn't. The dribbles of water ran down the wall too and at the top of the stairs in a puddle, lay tattered pottery and flowers.

I grabbed Davina and we crept down the stairs. I'm not sure who gasped. Maybe we both voiced the shock at seeing Olivia lying in a heap at the bottom of the stairs, a trickle of blood coming from her head . . .

Courtney Reynolds (13)
St Chad's Catholic High School, Runcorn

Manic

The shadowed figure continued to chase me through my father's cornfields. I could see his shadow in the moonlight, becoming ever closer to me, his knife outstretched in front of him. I turned left, still in the cornfields, trying to lose the manic creature: he continued to wail.

I started to wonder whether my parents were home, whether they had noticed I had gone and would come to my rescue. I noticed dark markings on some flattened corn. I decided to follow it. Fear etched into my heart.

After following the trail for about 10 metres, I came to an opening in the corn. The figure seemed to be off my track. I walked further into the flattened crop circle . . .

I saw the bodies of my dead parents and my little brother. My mother's legs were missing, as was some of my father's face. I was too scared to move. The moonlight shone on their partially eaten bodies.

What should I do? I asked myself. I heard rustling behind me, but put it to the back of my mind, thinking it was the wind. Suddenly, two claw-like hands grabbed my waist. I screamed and the hands turned me around. I was face to face with my family's murderer. It was clearly a man, with yellowing skin and cat-like eyes. His lips were red, presumably with blood. He took a knife out of his pocket, placed his hand over my mouth, and aimed for my heart.

Raechel Travis (14)
St Chad's Catholic High School, Runcorn

Believer

Do you ever wonder what those unexplainable, creepy noises are that you hear, more often when you're alone? Maybe you hear those noises when you're alone for a reason!

'The believer' is a small, crafty creature that lives in your home! It uses your belief to attack, so if you believe it exists, it'll make your darkest fear reality! You may think that your own house is the safest place to be, but you'd be wrong.

Rajiv was a boy who was told this story and believed!

Rajiv was twelve and for the first time, his parents decided to leave him at home alone.

The clock struck nine and Rajiv heard something between the floorboards. It sounded like a mouse running. Rajiv decided to take a bath, but Rajiv didn't realise that his deepest fear was drowning!

Suddenly, Rajiv slipped under the water and couldn't get up. He struggled anxiously. With all his effort, he managed to get out of the water. His parents came home. Scared and shaken, he got dressed and went downstairs!

Rajiv didn't tell his parents what had happened because he knew they wouldn't believe!

'The believer' was furious! It decided to strike again, and it succeeded!

Rajiv's parents arrived home and found no trace of Rajiv and nothing to prove that he'd ever existed.

Emma Cattrall (14)
St Chad's Catholic High School, Runcorn

Cassiopeia

The story starts in a village in the middle of a mountain. It was covered in flowers and fruit trees. The queen was a radiant woman, Cassiopeia. She was beautiful. All the men would fall at her feet just to be near her, but Cassiopeia was vain! She knew she was pretty and didn't mind showing herself off. Everybody knew that Cassiopeia thought highly of herself.

One day she was walking, looking for a new mirror. She spotted a former lover of hers and, as a bit of entertainment, decided she would make him fall in love with her again. She started to flirt with him, but it all went downhill when the man, Angus, said that a lovely lady, Edwina, had already captured his heart. This angered Cassiopeia so much! No woman could be prettier than her!

Cassiopeia decided to do something. She went to visit the strange men of the village - men who had been exiled.

Cassiopeia arrived at the cave and knocked on the stone. An old man hobbled out and lifted his hand to point inside, so she walked in. She explained her situation and asked for a curse to be put on Edwina. The men agreed, but asked to be allowed back in return. Cassiopeia rushed back to her palace.

The deed was done. Edwina looked horrid and Cassiopeia was back with Angus, but she forgot her agreement. As punishment, the strange men placed her upside down in the sky because of her vain ways.

Hayley Meagher (13)
St Chad's Catholic High School, Runcorn

A Day In The Life Of A Soldier At War

Dear Diary,
 I woke up this morning, it was very cold, wet and miserable outside. Me and my friends went to get some food, but due to our rations, there was not much at all to eat or drink.

 As soon as all us soldiers were awake, we had our morning drills. We were told to exercise, and then in groups we had to practise reloading cannons and guns.

 I have made many friends during this period of time. However, I'm missing my family greatly and although we are allowed to send letters, it's not the same as having an actual conversation.

 I remember the day that we heard that there was an opportunity to fight in the war. If I had the choice now, I don't think I would have raced to sign up like I did.

 This period of time here at war has been like a long dream and I haven't woken up yet. It has been so long and boring. All I have to entertain me are my war friends. I've already lost a few due to poor lack of defence by us.

 As part of this experience, we always have to be ready and aware of what might be waiting for us around the corner. So far, we haven't had our big war, all that has happened are little bullets being shot across into our trenches.

 This is the end for today, so I'll update you again tomorrow.

Laura Dixon (14)
St Chad's Catholic High School, Runcorn

A Day In The Life Of A Mistreated Horse

I seemed to be struggling through thick, slimy grass, sucking, deadly. I reared, trying to pull my feet free, and there was a crack, accompanied by a sharp pain through my skull.

As my vision cleared, I realised that in my nightmare, I had hit my head on the low shed ceiling. The slimy grass had in fact been the fetlock-deep layer of filth and manure that had built up over the weeks we had been there.

I glanced at the two silhouettes, shifting in the darkness. Two? I stiffened as I looked down at the roan Shetland pony, eyes vacant in death, his body a ghastly promise of our own fate. Shuddering, I sniffed the other two members of my motley herd. The tall, pregnant mare returned my query with an encouraging nicker, but the bay gelding barely blinked at us, his body sagging and broken, too far gone to notice.

After a few hours of kicking the shed door, it collapsed. The tiny, muddy paddock, devoid of grass, was little better than our shed, but we had not been out in two days. The gelding, however, folded his legs and fell into oblivion.

I shambled in circles for what seemed like an eternity, before coming to a decision. The weakening fence would be easy to push through. The mare fell in behind me. I pushed at the structure and it splintered as we both leapt forward, free at last!

Clare Wells (13)
Stockport Grammar School, Stockport

It Was The Weirdest-Looking Object I'd Ever Seen!

I rolled over onto my back and stretched out on my untidy, yet comfortable, bed. *Boring.* I wanted something to do. It's only the first week of the summer holidays and I was *already* bored.

'Kate, I'm just popping to town for a bit of shopping. I'll be half an hour or so,' I heard Mum call from downstairs.

I listened to the front door slam. I was just about to let out a sigh of boredom for the second time when I suddenly remembered: the attic. *While Mum's out, I can search the attic!*

The attic was forbidden to me and I was never given a reason why. So I decided to occupy myself with snooping around the attic to see what it was Mum and Dad were hiding from me.

I leapt excitedly downstairs to the garage and staggered back up the stairs with a ladder. I climbed gingerly up and opened the trapdoor. Sneezing every so often (thanks to the dust), I managed to scramble my way into the attic. Cobwebs hung everywhere. I drew away from them and started looking for whatever was being kept a secret from me. The floorboards creaked eerily below my feet. At first, I didn't find anything, but then I caught sight of an old cardboard box. It was very dusty and had been shoved into a corner. I rummaged through it and at the bottom of the box, there it lay. 'Whoa!' I breathed, staring in awe at it. I picked it up carefully and turned it over and over. It was the weirdest-looking object I'd *ever* seen!

Half an hour must have passed, because I heard the car turning in the driveway. *Mum!* Panicking, I started to throw all the ancient knick-knacks I'd been rooting through back into their boxes. But I wasn't quick enough.

'Kate, I'm home! Kate? Is that you up there?'

Natalie Ozel (12)
Stockport Grammar School, Stockport